PASSION

To Kay,

Best,

Cali Mackay

CALI MACKAY

Passion

The Billionaire's Seduction Series

By Cali MacKay

Copyright © 2015 by Cali MacKay

Published by Daeron Publishing

Http://calimackay.com

Printed in the United States of America

First Printing, 2015, edition 1.0 (links included)

ISBN: 978-1-940041-41-4

CHAPTER 1

Marshall **had always** been a calm and even-tempered man—but Claire was capable of pushing even a saint to commit murder. "I told you to take it up with my lawyer. And if you show up here again, I'll get a restraining order against you."

With a flick of her head, Claire gave him a smug look, her lips painted too glossy a red, her hair too perfectly coifed, and her fuck-me heels impossibly tall. How he'd ever fallen into her trap, he hadn't a clue. He might be a doctor, but he needed to get his goddamned head checked. "You can't, Marshall. Not when I deserve to be part owner of this company. And by the time my lawyer's through with you, you'll be lucky if I don't take everything you own away from you in the divorce. Just you wait."

"You don't own any part of this company until the courts say you do. So in the meantime, Claire—get the fuck out." Marshall couldn't believe she was going to try to steal his company from him, especially when she'd spent their time "together" screwing his friend and colleague at the hospital, while he busted his ass to build Clio from nothing.

He'd have never found out she was cheating on him, if it

hadn't been for one of his surgeries getting canceled at the very last minute. He'd come home to find her getting fucked on the dining room table by Dr. Luke Bingham. It'd been the final straw in what was already a miserable marriage, especially when he found out that they'd been sneaking around behind his back before they'd even said their marriage vows. That was probably the most infuriating part about it all: the fact that things between them had been nothing but a lie from the very start, doomed to fail.

And he fucking hated failure.

He just hadn't seen through her act until it was far too late—and it had truly been an Oscar-worthy performance. She'd set him in her sights from the moment she heard the word "doctor" and had milked it for all he was worth, playing the part of the doting girlfriend. Once they were married, she'd withdrawn and put the blame on him, even if he'd done all he could to make her happy—not that their marriage had ever stood a chance when it'd been nothing but a lie. And once he'd caught her cheating, she'd dropped the act and shown him the true person he'd married.

"So nice of you to use vulgarities when speaking to the mother of your child." She gave him a smug smile, one hand on her hip as she rubbed her belly with the other. "Because it is yours, Marshall. So you better be careful, or you'll never get to see your child. I'll make damn sure of it."

Rage and hatred roared in his chest, even as doubt and confusion clouded his mind. Had he really been stupid enough to sleep with her again? He couldn't fucking believe he'd do such a thing. Not in a million years after what she'd put him through.

But the truth was, he didn't remember much of that night, and he half suspected he'd been drugged. She'd come over upset about the divorce and had seemed conciliatory and apologetic. They'd had a glass of wine because she'd wanted a drink, and then...he had no clue. He'd awoken in his bed the following morning with a killer headache, and Claire was nowhere to be found.

The last thing he'd have guessed was that they'd slept together. And maybe they hadn't. It could just all be a ploy to make his life miserable until he could prove that the child wasn't his. In all their time of dating and being married, she'd always insisted on using a condom. Would she really change her ways? Unless her plan had been to get pregnant.

"I'm done arguing with you, Claire. I've already wasted too many years on you, and I'm not going to waste another fucking day." Marshall picked up the phone and called security, not wanting to risk putting his hands on her even if it was just to escort her out of the building, since he knew she'd somehow twist it around in the courts. "Security is on their way, so unless you want them to physically drag your sorry ass out of here, I suggest you get moving under your own steam."

"That's fine, since this place will be mine soon enough." With a glare, she hiked her designer purse higher onto her shoulder, and headed for the door, yanking it open and plowing into the unsuspecting woman on the other side as papers went flying everywhere. "Watch where the hell you're going, you cow."

Furious, Marshall watched her go, before turning to Harper Jones, one of his engineers, who was kneeling on the ground trying to gather the papers that had strewn across the floor. With his heart racing, he crouched at Harper's side and helped gather what looked like the report he'd requested, though he knew it was nothing more than a ploy to see her again. He'd been making excuses to see her—to flirt with her—ever since she started working at Clio nine months earlier. "I'm so sorry about that. And so sorry about her rudeness too. Are you okay?"

"I'm sorry if I interrupted something." Harper stood, holding onto the pile as papers stuck out in every direction and would likely take an hour to sort.

He stood by her side, towering over her petite but curvy frame as he gave her a smile and tried to slow his thundering pulse. Harper had been a new hire for their engineering and manufacturing department, and with her degree from MIT and the innovative projects she'd worked on while there, she'd been a perfect fit for Clio—in more ways than one. She was a brilliant engineer—one of the best he'd come across—and her designs had left Marshall excited and feeling inspired for Clio's future, as long as Claire didn't mess everything up.

"You have no reason to apologize, Harper. Honestly. I'm just sorry you had to be on the receiving end of all that. Let me give you a hand with these." He helped her get the papers into an organized pile and then went on the hunt at his secretary's desk for something to keep them contained. "I don't quite know where anything is. My assistant moved to Texas to follow her dream of becoming a cowgirl, or some such thing, and the temp hasn't shown up yet."

"Amy, right? I didn't really know her but...wow... a cowgirl?" Harper stifled a laugh that lit up her grey-blue eyes as she tucked a strand of dark mahogany hair behind her ear. Marshall's pulse raced, just as it always did when Harper was close. The girl was a bombshell, and she'd caught his eye from the moment he first met her during her final interview—not that he'd pursued her so soon after his split from Claire.

Yet it hadn't stopped him from making excuses to run into her at company events or in the break room, chatting and flirting over coffee and donuts, even if he'd told himself to leave well enough alone. But with things well and truly over between him and Claire—not to mention the little fact that Claire had never been faithful—it was hard to ignore the fact that he wanted Harper, desperately, and even their simple flirtations had made him a hell of a lot happier than he'd been while married to Claire.

His smile kicked up as a delicious tension coursed through him, his cock immediately going hard with a mind all its own, even as he tried to focus on the conversation at hand. "I do believe she found 'true love' on some dude ranch when she went out there on vacation. But hey, I guess everyone's allowed to follow their dreams and happiness, right? It's just left me rather short-staffed at the moment."

The temps were either more concerned about updating their profiles on social media or were appalled at the idea of working for a sex toy manufacturer—even if their products were high-end. "The temps the agency sent over haven't been great, though I half suspect my ex is either bribing the company or the temps in another attempt to make my life miserable."

Not that a simple assistant would truly fit the bill. Though he needed someone to manage his calls, emails, and all the day-to-day stuff—he also needed someone he could bounce ideas off of, someone to discuss the products and the industry and who'd be able to give him an educated opinion when he need it. He needed a personal assistant who would help him hone his ideas and help him focus where to take the company next—and not for the first time, he thought Harper would be perfect for the position.

"Wow...that seems pretty underhanded of your ex to screw with every aspect of your day." Not that Harper looked surprised that Claire could be behind that sort of ploy.

"I'm sorry—I must be taking up your time. Are these the design reports for the new Clio product line?" He held out his hands, offering to take the papers. Instead, she turned to what had once been his assistant's desk, and dug around the drawers, pulling out a giant metal clip.

"They are. And you're the boss, so if anyone's allowed to take up my time, it'd be you, right?" Giving him a smile over her shoulder that made him want her all the more, she efficiently sorted the papers into a few piles and then compiled them. His gaze drifted from her smile down to her slender waist, before lingering on her plump ass as she clipped the papers together. "There—that clip should hold better than the one I'd used originally."

"Well, I doubt you'd planned on literally running into my ex-wife." Because Claire was most certainly his ex as far as he was concerned, even if the divorce hadn't been finalized because she was dragging things out. He managed a smile, despite feeling frustrated with Claire, and then took the papers Harper was handing him. "Thank you, Ms. Jones."

"I'll let Todd know you have the reports. I'm sure he'll want to speak to you about the designs. Don't know if Todd mentioned it to you but...I was working on a bit of a side project. Thought it might work well with this latest design, so I made some notes. It's just an alternative method for developing vibrations that would provide...deeper stimulation. Anyway, it's all there. I'm sure Todd will schedule a meeting with you to go over it all." She started to go, when he stopped her with a gentle hand on her arm, unable to resist the urge to touch her. She turned back to him with a hopeful smile. "Was there anything else?"

"No, I suppose not, though I might have questions for you once I've read through your report." He told himself it was just work. Nothing more. Except that he knew he was lying to himself. It'd been too long since anyone truly piqued his interest, and Harper had most certainly done just that, right from the very start.

"Okay. Well…just let me know. I'm happy to go over the designs with you or answer any questions you have." She gave him a wave and then walked off, leaving him to watch the sway of her hips, his cock already hard, urging him to go after her, to pursue something more. But then she slipped around the corner with a final glance in his direction, a smile still on her lips.

Promising himself to do something about Harper, even if it was just a one-time thing to get her out of his system, he sat down at his desk. After a quick call to the temp agency for a more permanent solution, he then went through the project reports before turning his attention to Harper's idea for a new sort of vibe.

Although he'd started his studies as an engineer before switching to pre-med, Harper's designs were well over his head, though he got the general gist of it—and it was brilliant. Most vibes on the market used the same method for delivering vibrations, but this was a completely new approach—which was exactly what Clio needed.

As of late, it seemed like their competitors' designs were looking far too similar to their own. But Harper's new vibration method…it was perfect, especially if he could incorporate it into his own latest designs. He just had to make sure he kept it under lock and key, and maybe, just maybe, Harper was exactly what he needed to keep them ahead of the pack. Not to mention, with her brilliant mind, fuckable lips, and curves that he couldn't get off his mind, her designs weren't the only thing he wanted from the amazing Ms. Harper Jones.

Somehow, he managed to push her from his mind long enough to get a bit of work done, when there was a knock at his door and his brother let himself in. "Hey, Keane. I wasn't expecting you to come in today."

Though Marshall and his brothers didn't need to work after having inherited a sizeable amount of money, Marshall couldn't bear not working, and it seemed as though the same could be said for his brothers. Keane had decided to take on some of the marketing at Clio, and had been doing a damn good job of it, though he often worked from home. But given that there was a mole among them, Marshall was glad to have Keane around, knowing he could always trust his brother to have his back.

"I just wanted to drop off some of the latest packaging designs and ads we'll be running on targeted sites—and to see if you want company at the conference next week." The mischievous look in Keane's eye told Marshall all he needed to know—that his brother was looking to get himself into some trouble at the sex toy and adult novelties convention in London.

"What I need is for you to keep an eye on things here while I'm gone, especially with everything that's going on. Work with IT on this to go through emails, logs...whatever it takes. And if you think it necessary, get in touch with Quinn Ryker. His brother's fiancée runs a top-notch security firm." It pissed Marshall off to no end that someone within their company might be a mole, especially when he'd gone out of his way to make sure his employees were happy, well-compensated, and had every perk imaginable, from a full gym with a pool to gourmet coffee and donuts, not to mention great health insurance, a matched 401k, a casual atmosphere, and plenty of paid vacation time.

Though they were a sex toy manufacturer, there was an awful lot of money to be made, and the market was only growing as women became empowered and got more comfortable exploring their sexuality and taking ownership of it. Sex was no longer as taboo a subject. But that also meant that the sex toy industry had become lucrative, and whenever there was money involved, there were people willing to act less than honorably—hence the thefts of their designs.

Keane ran a hand over his thick stubble, his blue eyes jumping out in contrast to his dark hair. "Anyone you suspect?"

"If hate was the motivating factor, I'd say it's Claire, though she doesn't have access to anything of importance. That makes me think this is about money. Someone who's greedy or desperate." What made the mole even more difficult to find was the way they currently designed their products. Too many people and too many different departments had access to the designs before they went into production, and with money as the motivator, it could be anyone.

"I've got a bit of time, so I'll certainly look into it further. Try to figure out a way to contain the problem and with luck, maybe narrow it down to a few suspects so you'll have someone to question when you get back." Keane tilted his head towards the designs he'd brought over and then started getting to his feet. "Let me know if you need any changes made to those—and go home. You've been spending far too many late nights here. Just because you don't have Claire to go home to doesn't mean you can't find someone else to warm your bed and keep you entertained."

It was a pretty sad state of affairs when his baby brother was giving him advice on his love life. But he knew Keane had a point. Since everything went to hell with Claire, he'd been all work and no play, and he was tired of being a dull boy.

With that thought rattling in his head and it nearing the end of the day, he called down to engineering, hoping Harper had a moment to go over her designs with him, and perhaps entertain a few other...projects. Luckily, it wasn't long before she was knocking on his open door.

"Thanks for coming to see me." Needing to close the distance between them, Marshall came around and leaned against the front of his desk as she took the chair before him. "I know you're heading home soon, so I promise not to take up too much of your time. It's just that I had a chance to go over your designs, and I really like your idea for providing a different type of vibration and stimulation."

"Really?" Her smile lit up her eyes, and there was something so genuine and honest about her. It was a refreshing change after dealing with Claire for so long. "That's great. If you'd like, I can put together a prototype, and then once it gets your approval, I can hand it over to design so they can implement it."

"That would be perfect." Not that he was ready to let her go just yet. Anything to keep her around just a little longer. "Out of curiosity, what do you think of our current product lines? Are there any changes you'd make? Anything you don't like?"

She was in her mid to late twenties, which meant there was a good chance she had her own collection of sex toys, especially with the generous employee discount. It wasn't an unreasonable question, given her position within the company, and if she was smart enough to think of a new method for delivering vibrations, he wanted her opinion— and it had nothing to do with the fact that he wasn't quite ready to let her go yet.

"I think the current line is in keeping with the brand we've built so far." She bit her bottom lip as a blush crept across her cheeks, giving her pearly skin a rosy glow that made him want to cup her face in his hands and cover her mouth in a hard kiss.

It probably wasn't the wisest of ideas when he was her boss, but he'd been fighting the attraction between them for far too long. After dealing with Claire's craziness, he needed an escape, and Harper had caught his eye from the very first time she smiled in his direction.

He may not have been ready to truly pursue her back then. But now? He was well over his marriage and the lies Claire had told him, and he was ready to start living his life again. Pursuing Harper may not be appropriate, but he was beyond caring of what others thought if he could find a glimmer of happiness.

"Our latest designs might be in keeping with our brand, but are they innovative enough? I want to keep pushing the envelope—and I need to know if we've done that with our latest line. We need to always stay a step or two ahead of the competition." Unfortunately, that was becoming harder and harder to do when the competition was stealing their designs.

"I honestly don't know. I only help to figure out the mechanics once the design is finalized, but I don't have any say in the design itself." She gave him an apologetic shrug.

"But if you did have a say in the design, is there anything you'd change?" They had focus groups, but given Harper's work experience and education, he was hoping she'd have a new take on it—just like he'd approached the design of his vibes by using his knowledge of the human body as a doctor. It was what set Clio products apart from the competition. "What do you like in the vibes you use? What gives you the most pleasure?"

Harper's cheeks went from a simple blush to flaming red, and he knew if he were to brush her cheek, her soft skin would be hot to the touch. "I wouldn't really know. I hate to say it, but I haven't used our products, and...no offense, but it's not something I usually discuss—especially not with my boss."

Marshall's brows shot up as he tried to decipher exactly what she was saying. "I'm sorry. Do you mean you just haven't tried our products, or...you've never tried any sex toys at all?"

She let out a frustrated sigh. "I'm not saying I've never used them, it's just that...I'm sorry...how is any of this important?"

"It's important if you're helping to design them, don't you think?" Though he loved to see her blush, he wasn't trying to embarrass her. His concerns were valid—and it had nothing to do with the fact that his cock was forever hard in her presence.

"It is important. You're right, of course." She steeled herself, standing a little taller as her eyes met his, even if he could see her breath catch and her nipples go hard against the delicate silk of her blouse, their discussion clearly having an effect on her. "I'll be sure to acquaint myself more thoroughly with the products. Was there anything else you needed? I really need to get back so I can finish my work and wrap up for the day."

Marshall's lips quirked into a smile. "Actually, there is one more thing, Ms. Jones."

CHAPTER 2

Harper tried to remind herself that the sexy god of a man standing before her was her boss, and the conversation they were having was nothing but work. He wasn't flirting with her, even if her silly schoolgirl crush made her want to believe otherwise.

It had been so incredibly long since she'd last been with anyone that her body's reaction to Marshall was always immediate each and every time they bumped into each other, the mere sight of him enough to send her pulse skittering. And today's conversation? Well, that had her heart rattling and her cheeks flaming red, even as she tried to push aside the guilt she always felt when she thought of someone other than Josh.

Doing her best, she tried to focus on work and what Marshall was asking of her. "One more thing?"

He gave her a smile that sent a tingling warmth through her body and right to her core, making her go wet with desperate need. "I'd like you to try our products and get back to me about each one. What you liked, didn't like, how we could make it better. General impressions. And you'll be reporting back directly to me. Pick a product, take it home, and come see me first thing in the morning. I'll speak to your supervisor about it."

"But..." She all but stammered as her mind raced, trying to find a way out of the assignment. How the hell was she supposed to go home, masturbate, and then come back and give Marshall a report, when she couldn't even have a conversation with him without blushing?

Marshall took her hand in his and hauled her to her feet so there was just a breath between them, her full curves brushing against him as her breath caught in her chest. He was so close, so muscular, so tall...and when he leaned in just a little more with his head bent to hers, it was all she could do not to kiss him.

With his mouth at her ear, his words and the warmth of his breath sent a tingling shiver of need down her spine and straight to her clit, making her wish he'd take her right then and there. "Tomorrow, Ms. Jones. And make sure you're capable of giving me a thorough report."

Harper sucked in a deep breath to try to steady her racing heart, but it only filled her head with his masculine scent, so it took every ounce of willpower she had not to lean into him, not to tangle her fingers in his hair and cover his mouth in a greedy kiss.

Somehow she managed to string a few words together on a ragged breath, making it impossible for her to disguise just how bad she wanted him. "As you wish."

What the hell had she gotten herself into?

When Ben, one of her engineering friends, had landed a job working for Titan Adult, one of Clio's competitors over in California, she'd thought he was insane—until he told her that Clio was hiring in her neck of the woods. The easy commute, great pay, and amazing benefits had made it an easy decision for her, especially when the economy was still rocky and jobs were hard to come by.

Still...giving her smoking hot boss a full rundown of how she got herself off with their products hadn't exactly occurred to her when she'd read the job description. Still, she knew Marshall's point was a valid one. How could she be great at her job if she didn't have a full understanding of their products and hands-on experience?

Harper's pulse still hadn't settled by the time she got home that evening. Marshall had left her feeling frazzled in more ways than one, and one thing was certain—her body clearly didn't care that Marshall was her boss.

The moment she was through the door, she was forced to abandon her "assignment" and her dinner on the kitchen counter, as her cat, Moose, wound around her feet, attempting to trip her up in a demand to be fed. With a sigh, she popped open a tin of food for her giant Maine Coon, and then grabbed her Thai takeout, spooning the rice and coconut yellow curry onto a plate.

Dr. Marshall Foley... The mere thought of him left her both turned on and more than a little frustrated with his assignment, even though she knew he had a valid point about her not being personally familiar with their products.

It wasn't as if trying their range of vibes hadn't been on her to-do list, though to be fair, her job focused on developing the internal electrical components—not the design of the vibrator itself. Not to mention, by the time she got out of work, checked in on her dad to make sure he was doing okay, and then finally got home, all she wanted to do was curl up with a good book or watch some TV.

It's not as if she needed to be reminded that she had a nonexistent love life. That was pretty hard to ignore when the only one waiting for her when she got home was Moose. As for sex? It'd been far too long...not since Josh, and that had been close to three years now. After a while, it sort of felt like that part of her body had just gone dormant. And she knew how pathetic that was.

She just hadn't quite found the strength to move on, even if she knew she had to. Maybe that's why she'd flirted with Marshall, knowing it was harmless since it'd never come to anything with him being her boss. Except that it was far too easy to get hooked on her little routine of flirting with him while she grabbed her morning cup of coffee and donut from the break room, or doing her best to bump into him during their workday. And look where that now landed her.

Though she might need a bit of a kick in the ass to get her sex life jumpstarted, it didn't mean that she wanted to go on a sex toy marathon and then discuss her findings with her smoking hot boss—not even her boss, but rather the owner and CEO of the entire company.

She groaned at the thought and finished off her dinner, which totally hit the spot with its spicy coconut sauce, savory chicken, crunchy vegetables, and sweet pineapple, and then turned on the TV in her cozy living room, doing her best to ignore her work assignment. She flipped through the channels, one after the other, but with her assignment hanging over her head, she just couldn't relax or get settled.

Mumbling curses, she grabbed the vibrator box out of her bag, knowing there was no way out of it, rustled up a pad of paper and a pen so she could take notes, and grabbed herself a hard cider from the fridge. Heading to her bedroom to complete her assignment, she plopped herself on the bed, half-wondering if she'd get paid overtime for getting herself off.

Though the vibe she'd grabbed before leaving the office had yet to go into production, they were also in the process of perfecting the packaging, so she made sure to take note of those details as well. She had to admit, this was not some cheap and cheesy joke store vibrator, with its clear outer package, announcing to everyone exactly the sort of tawdry item that was being purchased and would take a nuclear arsenal to free the contents inside.

Instead, this was a beautiful teal, dark grey, and silver box made of a thick satin cardboard stock, the color of it gorgeous, and the design modern. It made a clear statement that this was an item of luxury—even if it was a vibrator. Carefully, she slipped the top of the box off, and removed the silk bag housing the vibe. She knew they sold for several hundred dollars, and understood that at that price point, paying attention to every little detail was key.

She stripped down to nothing and hopped into bed, tossing the covers aside and jotting down a few quick notes on her impressions so far. Slipping the vibe out of the bag, she noted that the feel of the silicone was velvety soft to the touch. She'd handled their products before, but this was all proving to be a rather different experience.

Although the vibe was rechargeable, she liked that it came pre-charged for immediate use, rather than having to wait. And the color was vibrant and fun, matching the aqua on the outside of the box.

Amazingly enough, she had some lube—but was it the right kind? Luckily it was. She jotted some more notes. Maybe they could develop a lube specifically for use with their products. The last thing you'd want is to drop a few hundred dollars on an amazing vibrator and then ruin it because you used the wrong kind of lube. Maybe even include a few samples with the vibe.

The shape of the vibe was a bit peculiar, though she knew they had several different designs. It was still phallic in shape, but had two additional extensions for added vibrations and pleasure, in addition to a handle for thrusting. Truth was, the handle felt a little large, though there was a cutout so one could get a different grip on the vibe. It could definitely prove useful if it was used while playing with a partner—although she couldn't help but think of Josh's reaction if she'd recommended using sex toys while being intimate with each other. She knew he'd have taken offense, as if he needed help pleasuring her.

Pushing Josh from her thoughts just like he'd pushed her out of his life, she jotted down a few more notes. Although the vibe could be used remotely through an app for full customization of the settings, it also had a wireless remote in case your phone wasn't handy. Lubing up the vibe, she cursed Marshall under her breath and set about to complete her assignment, knowing she'd have to give him a full report in the morning.

Yet now that she'd thought of Marshall, it was hard to push him out of her mind. He was so tall, with broad shoulders and muscular arms, dark hair, golden brown eyes, and a gorgeous face, his strong jaw often covered in just enough stubble to make him look ruggedly sexy. The mere thought of him had her breath catching and her nipples going hard, her body now thrumming with a sexual energy that had her fantasizing about his touch.

So it was with thoughts of Marshall, and the fact that

24

she'd be reporting to him first thing in the morning, that she turned on the vibe. She knew one of the selling features of the vibe was just how quiet it was, and she couldn't help but feel a bit of pride, knowing that she had helped contribute to that part of the design. Despite the powerful vibrations, it barely buzzed above that of a whisper.

Still thinking of Marshall and all he must be capable of with that gorgeous body of his, she slowly slipped the vibe deep inside her, though in her mind, she couldn't help but imagine it was him, his cock, claiming her, fucking her...

The intense vibrations raced through her core and teased both her clit and the bud of her ass as the shaft of the vibe filled her, expanding to contour to her body—a feature that was unique to Clio products. The sensation of being filled in conjunction with the intense vibrations was overwhelming, but it was her thoughts of Marshall taking her, fucking her, making her come, that pushed her precariously close to that delicious edge.

She thought of that moment in his office when he was so very close to her, recalled the way his muscular body felt against hers, the way his masculine scent filled her head, the way his breath danced over her skin. But what if he hadn't stopped there? She could easily picture him lifting her onto his desk and hiking her skirt up, his cock long and hard as he filled her, fucked her, her body stretched tight around him as he took her hard and called her Ms. Jones with that deep and sexy voice of his.

Her orgasm tore through her as she cried out, still fucking herself with the vibe, though in her head, it was still Marshall pushing her over that delicious edge, making her come harder than she ever had before.

And then, biting back her cries, she fumbled with the

remote to turn it off, her body quivering and overwhelmingly sensitive as the vibe continued to torment her. There. Finally...the vibrations stopped as she lay back against her pillows to try to catch her breath and let the dying tremors of her orgasm fade away, before finally pulling the vibe free of her body.

And now she knew exactly why their products were so popular.

* * *

Harper was a ball of nervous energy as she approached Marshall's office, ready to give him her report, her findings neatly typed so that she could hopefully just drop it off without actually having to discuss the whole sordid affair. It wasn't that she was a prude—far from it—but her orgasms felt personal, not a topic for discussion with her boss, especially when she'd been crushing on him since she first started working at Clio. She'd never manage to discuss her orgasm without blushing every shade of crimson possible and stammering like a fool, especially when she'd been fantasizing about him while getting herself off.

She tucked a loose lock of hair behind her ear, and bit her lip with nervous energy, trying to ignore the fact that she'd taken extra care that morning with her hair and makeup, and had made sure to pick out an outfit that she thought complemented her...assets. There was little hiding the fact that she was short and had a generous share of curves, which reminded her of Marshall's ex and her rude comment, even though Harper was fine with her curves, thinking it made her look like a fifties pinup.

There was a new temp sitting behind the desk, though she barely looked up from her phone as Harper stood there. "I'm here to see Dr. Foley."

The temp set aside her cell and looked up at her with a disinterested look as the phone on her desk started to ring. "Is he expecting you?"

"He is. Name's Harper Jones." The phone continued to ring as the temp let out a sigh. "I can wait, if you need to get that."

Another sigh as she finally answered. "'Ello...Dr. Foley's...please hold." She then pressed a few buttons, finally getting Marshall on the other line. "Someone's here to see you." Back to Harper she said, "What's your name again?"

"Harper Jones." She listened to her name get relayed back to Marshall, and a moment later, his office door opened.

"Harper. Please come in." He stepped aside to let her through, before turning to the temp. "Hold all my calls. I don't want to be interrupted."

He closed the door behind them, and with his hand gently resting on the small of her back, he escorted her farther into his office. It was just the smallest of touches, but even that slight contact between them had her clit throbbing with need, making it nearly impossible for her mind to focus. She was so doomed.

Doing her best to steady her nerves, she handed him her report, managing a small smile. "I wasn't exactly sure what sort of information you wanted, so I tried to be as thorough as possible."

"I appreciate it. Have a seat, Ms. Jones." The way he said her name...it always did her in: at once so formal, yet so sexy, his voice deep and velvety.

So much for making a quick escape. She grabbed a seat,

and tried not to blush as Marshall flipped through her report, scanning the few pages she'd typed up. "I like that you've included potential modifications we could make. However...I don't see any details of your personal experience."

That was because she'd left all of that out of her report. She felt her cheeks flame, and knew she must be blushing. "It worked as one would expect."

Marshall leaned back on his desk, his gaze taking her in with quiet amusement—a sentiment she didn't share. "I would certainly hope so. But I wanted to know the details of your experience, and I want to know how I can make it better. I want to know how to give you a better orgasm, Harper."

Her cheeks felt so hot, she swore she'd burst into flames. The way he talked about wanting to give her a better orgasm was doing things to her body—things she had very little control over, especially when in her mind, he'd been the one making her come last night.

And then...there was her ever-present guilt over Josh, the wound on her soul that she swore would never heal. Yet, her body had a mind of its own, and with Marshall so close, his presence so commanding, she couldn't keep her reaction to him, to his words, under control. She felt her nipples go hard and strain against her blouse as a desperate need started to ache between her legs and she felt herself go wet for him. Which was bad...very bad.

She could not start thinking about her boss in those terms, even if it had been far too long since she'd last been with anyone, leaving her always feeling so alone. And with his desk right there, how could she not picture him fucking her on it after her fantasy just the night before?

She told herself to focus, because she had no doubt Marshall could read her every thought. "I did put my suggestions in the report."

He flipped through the pages, before turning his intelligent gold eyes on her, reminding her of a wolf that had its prey cornered and was taking its time tormenting it, before turning to the pleasurable task of slowly devouring it. "You noted improvements we could make to the packaging...to the device...and yes, tweaking the product may result in a better orgasm, but I want to know more. If you had been the one to design this product, what would you have done differently to guarantee you got the most mind-blowing orgasm possible?"

She honestly didn't know. But given how smoking hot he was with his golden brown eyes, chiseled chin, thick dark hair, and sexy voice, she swore if he said the word orgasm one more time, she'd start humping his leg.

He pursed his lips, clearly not happy with her lack of response. "Ms. Jones...is it that you don't have enough experience with sex toys?"

"It's been awhile, I guess." She shrugged and tried to will her nipples into inverting themselves before she poked his eyes out. "But in my defense, I was hired as an engineer and have been working on the internal configurations in order to achieve the specific designs requested by our design team—not to work on the designs themselves."

"That's all well and good, and I know you've done an amazing job with those configurations. But I'm a firm believer that each department should have a working knowledge of what the other is doing so that we can stay innovative. It's a competitive marketplace. We need to think outside the box, Ms. Jones—and I do believe that means another assignment is in order." His eyes narrowed with humor as he took her in. "Pick another toy and report back to me. And if your husband or boyfriend has any input, I'd like to hear that too."

She had to restrain herself from tossing her hands up in the air in frustration. "I don't have a boyfriend...nor do I have a husband." She pushed away the hurt, annoyed with Marshall that he was pulling up emotions she preferred to keep buried, especially when she was at work. "And no offense, but my sex life is my own personal business. Having to write a report every time I get myself off is sucking the joy out of the whole thing."

She half expected him to fire her, but instead he threw his head back and laughed. "Okay...I wouldn't want to be the one responsible for ruining your sex life. If anything, I was hoping to improve it."

She nearly groaned at his words. Why the hell did he keep saying things like that? Or was she the one with the horny, sexually deprived mind and body that kept reading more into his words than he was intending? "What would improve my sex life right about now would be getting an orgasm from someone who actually has a pulse, rather than something that requires batteries. Because, I'm sorry, but vibrators don't cuddle you to sleep after sex and then cook you breakfast in the morning. Not to say that our vibrators don't give mind-blowing orgasms. They do. And that's great if you're just looking to get off. But...I think I've said too much."

She got to her feet, hoping to make her escape, and already regretting everything she'd said. She desperately needed this job, and she may have just flushed her career down the toilet. Before she could head to the door, he grabbed her hand and pulled her to him, his strong arm wrapping around her waist.

"Don't go, Harper." He was suddenly so close, but...the hint of melancholy in his tone, not to mention that he'd used her first name instead of calling her Ms. Jones, had her softening in his arms. "Everything you said is true. It's much better if you have a partner to share the experience with."

"Not that that's always possible. Believe me—I get that." She hated feeling sorry for herself, but she missed having someone in her life to share her day with.

"Ms. Jones..." Once again, he smelled so good, she couldn't help but lean into him. And then he was merely a breath away when he bent his head to hers and caught her mouth in a heart-pounding, knee-melting kiss, his muscular body hard against hers as his tongue found hers and her hands fisted around the fabric of his shirt, pulling him even closer to her, her body desperate for so much more.

What the hell was she doing?

Somehow she found the strength to pull away, even if every nerve in her body was thrumming with need. "Marshall..."

"I suppose I shouldn't have done that." With his eyes locked on hers, he brushed her hair aside and then cupped the back of her neck. "Then again, I probably shouldn't do this either."

CHAPTER 3

Ignoring all sense, Marshall tangled his fingers in Harper's hair as he hauled her body against his, his mouth hard on hers, taking, tasting as his tongue swept over hers, his cock stiff and desperate to have her. Shifting her back, he lifted her onto the edge of his desk as she wrapped her legs around his thighs, pulling him close. It didn't matter that he was her boss, or that he knew better than to get involved with an employee. After thinking about her all night long, thinking about her getting herself off with the vibe…all he knew was that he'd never wanted anyone as bad as he wanted Harper in that moment.

Her grey tweed skirt hiked up her legs as he slipped a hand down her back, grabbing her ass to pull her close so her hips rocked against his cock as he nipped at her neck.

And then she put a hand on his chest and pushed him away, though the last thing he wanted to do was stop. "Marshall…we can't do this."

"Can't or shouldn't, Ms. Jones?" He took a deep breath to try to slow his heart and clear his head so that he wouldn't ravage her on his desk. And though she'd put a stop to things between them, she'd clearly been more than a little willing up until that point.

"Well, we're certainly both capable, though given the fact that you're my boss, I suppose shouldn't would be the proper answer." As she let her legs slip to the floor, her hips rode down his length, making him want her even more, leaving her trapped between his body and his desk—not that she was making any moves to go around him.

"I'm looking for an...assistant. Someone who'll give me a different perspective when it comes to dreaming up new product lines. Someone who'll inspire me and keep me innovating. And I want that person to be you, Harper." She'd be perfect for the job, since he was already feeling damn inspired. "I thought your new method for delivering vibrations was brilliant and I need that sort of thinking to keep my own ideas flowing."

"I'm glad you liked the idea, but I'm just an engineer. I wouldn't even know where to start as an assistant." She shook her head with a sigh, as if trying to clear it.

"And yet, you've already done brilliantly. I'm not asking for you to be my secretary—though believe me, I'm desperate for one. I'm asking you to be...my muse. I'm asking you to collaborate with me so we can keep Clio moving ahead of the competition." He gave her his most dazzling smile, hoping to sway her just a little. "I honestly think this is the perfect arrangement, Ms. Jones. And unless you have a reason to deny me, I'd like you to start first thing tomorrow. Take the day and wrap up any loose ends, and I'll make sure to speak to Todd."

"You know this is insane, right?"

All Marshall could do was shrug and give her a knowing smile as he saw her out. "What's seen by some as insanity is often a stroke of genius, Ms. Jones—and I'm counting on it being the latter."

***

Marshall knew he was taking a risk when it came to mixing business with pleasure, but at this point he didn't care. He was tired of innocently flirting with Harper and then letting her walk away without pursuing it further. Maybe the hellish divorce was frying his brain. Or maybe it was the fact that he'd found Harper intriguing from the very first moment he'd laid eyes on her.

As far as he was concerned, it was a miracle he'd managed to stay away for as long as he had, given that she was cute as a button and sexy to boot, even if he knew he was taking a massive risk. He'd never have been so bold or forward with any of his other employees, and he groaned at the thought of her accusing him of sexual harassment.

He suddenly felt like an ass, though he told himself that none of his requests had been unreasonable given the sort of company he was running. You had to be willing to discuss sex if you were going to work for a sex toy manufacturer, although he'd definitely crossed the line when he'd kissed her and then nearly fucked her on his desk—and he'd do it all over again, given half the chance.

It may be wrong, but he needed the sort of distraction Harper was offering him. With Claire trying to make every part of his life miserable, Harper had made him forget about his failure of a marriage, and she made him feel like his old self—before Claire had destroyed his trust with her lies.

At the moment, Harper was exactly what he needed—not just emotionally, but professionally. Seeing Harper's ideas and discussing them with her had reinvigorated him—

and he hadn't felt that way since he first started the company. She might not be completely sold on taking this new position, but he'd do whatever it took to make it happen, and to make sure she was happy.

Harper might be somewhat inexperienced when it came to sex toys, but Marshall was convinced she was just the sort of person he'd been looking for in an assistant. In a way, her inexperience could be a good thing, since it offered him a different perspective. Maybe they could tap into a new demographic, and find a way to appeal to women who were unsure or uncomfortable with vibrators.

By the time he got to work the next morning, he couldn't wait to get started, a newfound excitement thrumming through his body at the thought of getting to work with Harper, pleased that she'd finally agreed to work with him.

Harper was already waiting for him when he got to his office, though she still looked uneasy. "Don't look so nervous, Ms. Jones. I promise, I'll make sure you enjoy yourself."

The sexual innuendo may not have been intentional, but it was damn hard to keep his mind out of the gutter when she looked like a retro bombshell, wearing fitted navy capris, a pretty white silk blouse that showed off just enough skin to make him crazy, a pale pink cardigan, and sensible canvas sneakers. Although she might be overdressed for the casual work environment he offered his employees, it was perfect: at once dressy and casual with a style all her own.

"I'm still not sure what I'm supposed to help you do, or why I'm really here." She bit her bottom lip, looking worried and uncertain, and it took all the self-control he could muster to not kiss her worries away.

He should feel guilty for thinking it—but he didn't. His life was currently too fucked up for him to turn away from something that would feel downright amazing—and he had no doubt whatsoever that it would be just that. Unlocking the door, he led them into his office with a hand on her lower back, unable to resist the urge to touch her. "You're going to help me come up with our newest product line. Feel free to make yourself comfortable—though I should get you your own office. Adjoining to mine, of course, since that'll be easiest for work purposes."

"Honestly, I don't need much. Just a desk somewhere would be more than enough. But...I need to talk to you about my projects. I can't just up and leave my responsibilities when I'm in the middle of developing components my coworkers are going to need." She paced his office floor, her bottom lip caught between her pearly white teeth, her nerves clearly getting the better of her. Stepping into her path, he cupped her face, brushing his thumb across her cheek, hoping to soothe away her worries.

"Stop stressing out, Harper. I promise you it'll be fine. And if your team needs any help, I'll make sure they get it." Her eyes slipped shut as she took a deep breath, leaving him to wonder if there was more bothering her. "I know it may not have been the position you were hired for, but this is a great opportunity for you—and of course it'll give you a bump in salary."

She stepped away from his touch, shaking her head as if to clear it. "I can't risk ending up unemployed when you decide that you need to get back to running your company, and you've tired of having me around to contemplate products with. I have responsibilities outside of this job."

Is that what was bothering her? "Harper...your job is safe here. No matter what. But I honestly think this could be perfect. You've got the technical background I need—and you're great with taking a different approach to what's traditionally been done. You're wasted on putting together someone else's designs when you could be thinking up your own."

She held his gaze with hers and let out a deep breath. "You seem awfully sure of what I'm capable of."

"And you seem awfully uncertain of it." And that just wouldn't do. "What happened to make you question your abilities, Ms. Jones? Was it an ex-boyfriend? Your parents?"

"Don't. You don't get to psychoanalyze me—and my personal life is my own." She went back to pacing, though this time it was with an anger he hadn't anticipated.

"My apologies. I didn't mean to pry or be disrespectful." He'd clearly hit on a nerve, and the last thing he wanted was to make things worse between them. But when he saw her eyes shimmer with tears she was desperately trying to hold back, it made him feel like such an ass. Without a thought, he pulled her into his arms, desperate to make things right between them. "Hey...I'm sorry, Harper. I truly am."

Holding her close, hoping to be able to offer her some comfort, her body shuddered in his arms as she fought to get control of her emotions. It was clear that whatever had upset her clearly wasn't an easy matter for her.

Though she didn't pull out entirely of his arms, she did put enough distance between them to swipe away at the few tears that had escaped. "I hate this. You must think I'm such a drama queen."

"What I think is that you don't look like the type of

38

person to get emotional if it isn't for a damn good reason. But I also think you've probably been dealing with this problem on your own for far too long." He hadn't a clue as to what sort of problem she was dealing with, but she was always so put together and she didn't seem like the sort of person who came to tears easily. That could only mean that she was under a lot of pressure, and it was getting to be too much, especially with the added stress of changing jobs. "Maybe we need to get out for a bit…get some fresh air and a change of scenery."

She shook her head and took a step back. "But…there's work to do."

"And all that can wait until we've grabbed a cup of coffee, and maybe a bite to eat." With a firm grip on her shoulders, he spun her around and got her moving towards the door. "Have you had breakfast yet? We can talk business while we're out."

She looked up over her shoulder at him, looking more herself. "I don't suppose my banana counts when you're looking so determined."

"Not unless it was over a pile of pancakes, Ms. Jones." He knew just the place to take her. It was one of his brother's favorites and since Jake was a chef, he always knew of the hidden gems. "We're going to the Greasy Spoon."

Her lips quirked into a hint of a smile that eased the tension in his chest. "That sounds appetizing."

He barked out a laugh, especially since he'd had exactly the same reaction when Jake first brought him there. "The name's been there since the fifties, but the food is some of the best in the area, even if it is an old-school diner."

The drive along the shore to where the diner sat steps from the beach was relatively brief, and Marshall figured it'd be best to wait until they'd settled in before they got started on work. Seeing her upset had left him feeling protective of her, and though she was still his employee, he was treading into dangerous territory, clearly unable to help himself.

Whatever was bothering her, whatever she was having to shoulder, made him want to ease her burden, even if there was a little voice inside his head that told him this could be a grave mistake. After all, his entire relationship with Claire had started when she'd come to him with some damsel in distress story. He just couldn't resist swooping in to be the hero who saved the pretty girl.

Not that Harper was anything like Claire.

Marshall now knew that Claire had manipulated him from the very start, playing him beautifully, her performance Oscar-worthy. She'd seen him as a ride to an easy life, and she'd done everything possible to ensure he'd fall for her, even though he'd half suspected there was something wrong. And he swore, he wouldn't be fooled again.

This thing with Harper was completely different. It was just work—and a whole lot of fun, if she didn't get hung up on the fact that he was her boss. And right about now, he needed a bit more fun in his life, since his life was bordering on being a fucking disaster.

They gave Lois their order and it didn't take long for her to come back with coffee, his lumberjack breakfast, and Harper's Greek omelet. They munched silently for a bit, before he decided a bit of conversation was in order. "Did you take another product home last night, Ms. Jones?"

"No, I did not, Dr. Foley." She perked her brows at him scoldingly, and then broke off a piece of well-done bacon and popped it into her mouth, her eyes still locked on his. "If you need me to put together a testing panel, I'll happily do that."

"What I need is your opinion based on your own personal experiences. If you need help figuring things out, I'll gladly oblige you." Marshall knew he was skating on thin ice. She could easily take his offer the way he'd actually intended it—since he'd clearly lost his mind—or she could choose to take it as a professional offer to just show her the product in a non-sexual manner and setting.

She pinned him with a stare, her brows going from scolding to you did not just say that. "Pardon me?"

"If you can't figure out how to use the product, I'll happily go over the settings and remote with you." He then feigned mock horror. "Ms. Jones, you didn't think I meant…"

Her eyes narrowed as she pinned him with a knowing stare. "You mean after you kissed me in your office? I don't know why I'd possibly think such a thing."

"I may have been out of line when I kissed you. Given the industry we're in, it's hard for there not to be sexual innuendo with half of what we say when we're typically discussing things of a sexual nature. And I'm fully aware that it can sometimes lead to a sexually charged environment." He really was such an ass, and though he did want her, he'd never want her out of fear or obligation. "I hope you know that you don't ever have to do anything you're not comfortable with. There won't be any consequences to your employment. I mean that, Harper. And I need you to be honest with me if something I've said or done has made you feel uncomfortable—including that kiss."

"Well, I appreciate that, although it's not like I didn't kiss you back." She sat back in her seat, managing a reluctant smile. "That said, I still don't quite understand how I'll be of any help as far as this job's concerned."

"Sometimes, innovation requires inspiration—and that's exactly what I've hired you for. It requires thinking of things differently, taking a different approach. It's a rare thing, Harper—but I think you have that ability." He had to get her to see that she was capable of so much. "And I already think you might be onto something. Yesterday, you mentioned how you'd prefer a more human interaction with your orgasms. Well...we don't have a toy that can be used by both parties during sex—and would pleasure both parties. What's currently on the market has had mixed reviews, but I think we can do better, especially if we approach it from a different angle."

"I suppose." She gave him a bit of a nod, and he could see her thoughts churning in her head. "Should I talk to design about it? I'm sure they could come up with some prototypes."

"It can wait until we've explored the idea further. That way we'll have more of a direction to give them before they get started. But this is exactly why I want you working with me—so we can bounce ideas off each other." He gave her a smile, hoping she could see just how good their partnership would be. Although he hadn't mentioned his most recent idea for a vibe, he knew it could be a game changer since there was nothing else like it on the market—and Harper's technical background and questioning mind would be exactly what he needed to perfect his design.

She cut a piece of her omelet, a frown on her lips, and

her brow drawn in worry. "I think you're expecting a lot of me—and I guess I'm just worried you'll end up disappointed."

"Hey..." He tipped her chin up, forcing her to look at him, as he tried to control his anger. After a lifetime of living with a father who never saw anything his kids did as good enough, he was pissed off to see that sort of uncertainty in her. "You have this, Harper. So don't go doubting yourself."

She managed a smile. "You're a good man, Marshall."

He gave her a shrug and matched her smile with one of his own. "Maybe."

CHAPTER 4

"Well, I appreciate the vote of confidence—and your concern." Harper didn't quite know what to do about Marshall. He left her feeling completely off balance, especially when there was clearly more between them than just work. Nine months of flirting had all but guaranteed that. But now...he was offering her an amazing opportunity, and the last thing she wanted was to ruin it by complicating things with something physical, even if it was taking all she had to fight her attraction to him.

"Of course." He gave her hand a squeeze and a smile that reached his eyes so they glowed from within, like flickers of a flame caught in a glass of fine bourbon. "By the way, there's a tradeshow coming up in London and I want you to join me. We'll fly out this weekend, and will be there for five—maybe six days. Do you have a passport?"

Now that was one hell of a bad idea. Even though she had a passport, the last few years had left her with a fear of flying. But there was more... The thought of leaving her father to his own devices had her on edge. Her mom's death from cancer had devastated him, and he'd taken to self-medicating to ease his hurt.

"I don't know if I can go with you, Marshall. I have a...cat." She groaned, knowing how stupid that sounded.

"I'll send a pet-sitting service around—at my expense, obviously. Get anything else you might need. There will be some evening functions, so you may need something relatively formal. Other than that, general business attire should do. Here..." He dug a credit card out of his wallet and handed it to her, ignoring her protests when she tried to give it back to him. "And in the meantime, I think we could do with a bit of research."

Once they wrapped up with breakfast, Harper found herself sitting back in the soft leather seat of Marshall's SUV as he drove them into Portsmouth. She was unsure of where exactly he was taking them for "research," but she could just imagine. A sex shop? A sex club?

She wanted to groan. It wasn't that she was some virginal prude—she wasn't. She loved sex just as much as the next person. It's just that she preferred to keep things private rather than analyze them with a fine-toothed comb—with her boss. Especially when her sex life was nonexistent. After Josh...the truth was she'd been too heartbroken. Sex—or rather the lack of it—had been pretty far down on her list of problems.

She'd known she might be a bit out of her depth when she took the job at Clio, but the pay and benefits had been fantastic during an economy that was only just getting back on its feet. There had been few options for work, especially if she didn't want to eat up half her day commuting into Boston. With her needing to keep an eye on her dad, that just wasn't an option.

The truth was, she considered herself damn lucky to have landed her job at Clio. And maybe that was the reason she was feeling rather panicked that Marshall wanted her as his assistant. What if she didn't live up to his expectations and it jeopardized her position at the company? Would he let her go back to her old position or would he fire her? He said her job was safe, but was it really? It just wasn't something she could risk—even if she was finding it harder and harder not to fall for Marshall's charms.

It'd be a hell of a lot easier if he was some sort of conceited asshole—but he wasn't. He was sweet, considerate—even though he was constantly pushing her out of her comfort zone—and he was so sexy, it made her knees weak. Every time he touched her, kissed her, it was all she could do not to want more. It may have started as innocent flirting and a schoolgirl crush, but now? The flirting was now far from innocent, and she didn't even want to think of what might become of her crush if she let herself fall for him.

"So...how is it you're still single, Harper?" He glanced over at her with a sexy smile, his gaze lingering for a moment longer before turning back to the road.

"So...how is it you're getting divorced?" She hated to be forward or rude—but he started it.

Luckily he must have found her question entertaining, because he was laughing with a shake of his head. "Fair enough, Ms. Jones. I'm getting divorced because I was stupid enough to have married the wrong person. And since I didn't quite manage to figure that out on my own, she decided to give me a hand figuring it out by sleeping with one of my coworkers."

"Oh." There was nothing worse than that sort of betrayal. "I'm so sorry. That's just...rotten."

"Even more rotten was coming home to find them screwing on our dining room table—though in a way I'm glad for it. It finally allowed me to see what was really going on." His smile faded, and she couldn't blame him for being upset. "Anyway...that would be why I'm getting divorced. Your turn—how is it that someone as smart, and sweet, and pretty as you is still single?"

That was the last question she wanted to be answering, knowing it'd lead to the looks of pity, when she explained that she had once been engaged, but her fiancé had broken things off between them and pushed her away after his two-seater plane ran into engine problems. The crash left Josh partially paralyzed and in so much pain, he was now confined to a wheelchair, bitter and angry with the world.

Although Marshall had been honest with her, she couldn't quite bring herself to tell him what had happened. "I've just been busy with work, and I'm not really the sort to hit clubs and bars. Besides, actively looking for a partner, like on a dating site, just feels odd to me. I guess I figure it'll happen organically if it's meant to be."

"We don't work you that hard, do we?" He parked the car and shifted to face her, his eyes alight with humor and mischief, though being on the receiving end of his intense gaze had her squirming in her seat as her body reminded her that it'd been far too long since a man had touched her. "Or is it the recent late-night assignments?"

She shook her head with a laugh. "I can't believe we're back to that."

"Well, you'd think that your lack of a boyfriend might have you more willing to give our products a try. So why isn't that the case?" When she narrowed her eyes at him, he put his hands up as if in defense. "And before you start thinking that this is just me prying into your sex life...well, I suppose it is in a way, but only because it makes me think that there are plenty more women like you out there, and if we can tap into that market, it'd be a goldmine."

"Women like me, huh?" Harper couldn't resist teasing him, though she did wonder exactly what category he'd just stuck her in. "You have me curious as to what you think my demographic is."

"Young, smart, educated, gorgeous, smoking hot, and single." He reached over and brushed her cheek, sending her heart skittering inside her chest. "There's a tension in you...a sexual energy coursing just below the surface, waiting to be unleashed."

Her breath caught, even as she somehow managed to keep her voice steady. "Is that so? And you're the one to unleash it, are you?"

Marshall leaned in and nuzzled her, brushing his lips against hers in a whisper of a kiss. "I'd like nothing more, Ms. Jones. Though I suspect you know that already."

He then pulled away from her with a smile, exiting the car and coming around to get her door, leaving her smoldering from that kiss as her imagination filled in the blanks on what could come next if she gave in to what was between them. "Where are we going?"

"There's a high-end sex boutique I want you to check out. The owner is a good friend and was great for bouncing ideas off of when I was first starting up Clio." He slipped his hand down to the small of her back, letting it rest there as he escorted her up the steps to the pretty little boutique.

Her heart was still racing from that kiss, and it certainly didn't help that her mind kept replaying it on an endless loop. With his hand lingering on her waist so she could feel his fingers splayed out protectively, it was hard for her not to want more from him. Which was downright insane, given that he was her boss. Not to mention he was in the middle of a nasty divorce.

Harper had heard the rumors about how his wife had ambushed him at Clio's black-tie charity event and announced to the world that she was pregnant with his child and how she'd never let Marshall see it. Every part of her orderly and responsible mind told her to stay the hell away from him. Yet her body clearly had a mind of its own, as if it were finally protesting her complete lack of a sex life—and at this point her need for him was strong-arming her brain and completely overriding anything that made sense, as long as it resulted in Marshall's hands on her neglected body, and his mouth hard on hers.

It'd been three long years of missing Josh, of missing his smile and his infectious laugh, three years of trying to make things right between them, of trying to reach out to him only to have him push her away and refuse to speak to her. Three years of letting her life pass her by, of hoping he might someday find the person he'd been before the horrific accident that had nearly claimed his life. Yet she had grown tired of the guilt, tired of the loneliness, and though she still missed him, she was desperate to walk away from the darkness and back into the light once more. And at that very moment, it felt a lot like Marshall was offering her his hand so he could lead her to a brighter, happier place—and she was more than ready to clasp it and never let go.

Steeling herself for whatever might come her way, Harper stepped into one of the prettiest shops she'd ever seen, the décor and colors reminding her of a Parisian boutique, despite the sex toys on display. A pretty woman in her early forties stepped out from behind an antique desk and greeted Marshall warmly with a kiss on his cheek that he returned. "It's been too long, Marshall."

"It has." Stepping to the side, Marshall gave Harper a warm smile and made the introductions. "Aria, this is Harper. She's a brilliant engineer who's working with me to develop a new line of product. Harper, this is Aria, the friend I was telling you about."

"It's a pleasure. It's rare for Marshall to bring anyone with him—he must be really excited about this new line. So what are you kids working on?" Aria hooked Harper's elbow with hers and shifted them farther into the shop, the intimate gesture at once sweet and yet odd for someone she'd just met.

"We're thinking of a new line of toys that could be used by couples." Marshall wandered about the shop, browsing through the toys—and there were a lot of toys, not to mention there was a variety of other items, from gorgeous lingerie to products aimed towards more of a BDSM crowd. "What do you currently carry, Aria?"

"These right here..." Aria let Harper go, and shifted behind a glass case where a variety of toys where elegantly displayed and highlighted under lights. "As I'm sure you know, there isn't a whole lot out there. These here are the only ones really worth carrying, and even then, they're not for everyone. Some people love them, but others have said they're uncomfortable, or the vibes aren't quite strong enough, so I'll be curious to see what you come up with."

Marshall stepped to Harper's side as he gently leaned on the counter, his hand once more returning to the small of her back. "If you could pack us up one of each, that would be great. And...is there anything else you're currently fond of?"

"You mean other than your products?" She gave him a flirty smile and a shrug, leaving Harper to wonder if their relationship had ever extended past that of friendship. Marshall may have been married, but she doubted he'd been a virgin on his wedding night. "Honestly, there hasn't been anything new as far as vibes go. However, this here..." She grabbed a small silver tin from behind a different counter and put it in front of Marshall. "This here can give a woman mind-blowing orgasms. It's basically a balm that heats up and sensitizes everything. Problem is, it's not really safe to use with some of the toys."

"If you could add a few of those to my bill, that would be great." Marshall turned to Harper with a smile. "Is there anything you'd like? Anything you think might help spark some ideas?"

"Actually...yes. These vibrating cock rings...is it just these few here?" Given that this was a high-end sex boutique, the selection was limited to just the best products and quality, but Harper hadn't realized just how few high-end cock rings there were. She knew Clio didn't carry one as of yet, and thought it might be another product they could pursue.

"Unfortunately. The rest of them tend to be made of horrible material and are no more than a bullet vibe stuck in some jelly." Aria wrinkled her nose, clearly appalled at the thought. "Obviously, those aren't anything we'd ever carry. If you give me a minute, I'll put all this together for you, unless there's anything else?"

"Add the cock rings—and anything else you think we might find interesting." Marshall waited until Aria slipped into the back room, and then, grabbing Harper's hand, pulled her to him and slipped a strong arm around her waist, catching her mouth in a passionate kiss. "I can't wait to get to work."

"Work being the key word there, Marshall." At least she was trying to behave herself, saying all the things she should be, even if her body was leaning into him, desperate to have him kiss her again. "Or have you forgotten that you're my boss, and this could easily be considered sexual harassment by some."

"Am I harassing you, Ms. Jones?" He tightened his hold on her, making it impossible for her to ignore his massive hard-on as he fisted her hair with his free hand and pulled her head back so he could nip his way down her jawline to her ear and then her neck. "If you want me to stop, by all means tell me, and I'll stop. But if you don't, then I think it's time we give up this charade of you not wanting me. Because you do want me, Ms. Jones...don't you?"

All she could do is groan in response. Curse him.

"Shall I take that as a yes? Or should I find out for myself?" He nuzzled her until she couldn't help but kiss him, her body coming to life for the first time in a very long time, her need erasing her guilt, so that by the time he pulled away, her breathing was heavy and her knees were threatening to buckle on her. "There's a good girl."

She couldn't believe him—couldn't believe that she'd somehow succumbed to his charms. "You've got some balls, Marshall."

His smile kicked up as he kissed the tip of her nose. "Among other things, princess."

CHAPTER 5

Marshall knew he was playing a dangerous game when it came to Harper, but in his defense, he had never in all his life crossed the line with an employee or coworker. So then, what the hell was his problem? At least the chemistry between them seemed to be mutual, even if Harper was hesitant. Not that he could blame her, given their circumstances.

Back at Clio headquarters, he let them into his office, half-wondering where his temp was, since once again there was no one at the desk outside his office. Something would need to be done—starting with a new agency.

Due to the late nights he too often spent in his office, he'd designed himself a comfortable seating area, which came in handy just now as he settled them in on the soft leather sofa, instead of attempting to work at his desk.

"Let's start with the vibes for couples." Marshall dug through their shopping bags and laid out on the coffee table all the toys designed for couples.

Harper started to pull them out of their boxes, taking care to line up all the packaging and components with the matching device. Given that these were all high-end products, the packaging on each was decent, at the very least, though Marshall had taken special care with his own product lines to make sure they immediately spoke of luxury.

Holding up one of the couple's vibes, Harper wrinkled her nose at it. Shaped like a U, each end was bulbous with a vibrating tip and was designed to have one end inserted so that it hit a woman's G-spot, while the other tip stimulated her clit. Though it could be used on its own, it was actually designed to be worn during intercourse. "Is it just me or does this look like it might be uncomfortable once you have it inserted along with your partner thrusting into you?"

"It is rather bulky, though I'd imagine that probably helps with that full feeling that some women like." Though he wasn't sure how comfortable it'd be to have his cock rubbing against it. "From a guy's perspective, though, I'm not sure how pleasurable it'd be."

Harper's brows perked up in amusement, as if suddenly his lack of experience with the device somehow validated her own inexperience. "Do you mean to tell me that you haven't tried this sort of toy before? Dr. Foley, I do believe you've been slacking off on your research."

"You, my sweet, have no excuse for not using toys designed to give a woman pleasure. I, on the other hand, haven't been with anyone since filing for divorce, and these products are relatively new. Given that they're designed for a couple, I do believe that I have a valid reason for my lack of experience with the product." Marshall thought of offering her an evening of research—in his bed, of course—but worried it'd be a little too much, too soon, and given that they'd be working together, he had time to be a little more patient.

"I think the idea of stimulating the clit and G-spot are good ones on the woman's end, but do vibrations really help stimulate the guy and give him pleasure? There's just got to be a better way to design this, though it might require a different method for producing vibrations. One that wouldn't result in something so bulky." She chewed her lip, looking deep in thought as she turned the device around in her hand. "This one also doesn't come with a wireless remote, which means it could be a bit of pain to change through the different settings once it's in use, although some of the others are wireless."

"Regarding the vibrations from a man's perspective, it can certainly help things, but only if it's not making things uncomfortable. But there's also the issue of size. Some men are more generously endowed, and women can also vary in how tight they are. For our vibrators, we were able to overcome that difficulty by making the girth of the shaft expandable. We could use a similar technology, starting out with something rather slim." It was something to mull over at the very least.

The others weren't terribly different in design, and after a bit of discussion on the various advantages and disadvantages of each product, he decided to pick up the item she'd been most curious about. The vibrating cock ring. "Do you have any sort of experience with cock rings?"

The way she blushed had him thinking she did have a partner who'd worn one for her—although the thought of her with another guy fucking pissed him off to no end, even if he had no right to feel anything remotely close to jealousy. "The way I see it, it prolongs everyone's pleasure, and though it might not hit her G-spot, the vibrating extension will stimulate her clit. With some modifications...we could make sure the guy got a bit more out of it too. Maybe add another band with a vibrating plug that sat behind the man's balls, hitting that sensitive spot—or with an extension that could be inserted anally."

Suddenly, his innocent little scientist seemed a lot less innocent—and he fucking loved that bit of juxtaposition. He picked up the balm Aria had liked and opened it, quickly realizing it was unlike most lubes on the market. It was more the consistency of lip balm, and as he ran his fingers over the smooth surface, the heat of his touch melted it just enough to coat his fingers. There was a nice herbal and citrusy smell to it, and it felt great on his skin. As he massaged it, the balm warmed up with a tingly heat, and he quickly realized why Aria liked the product so much.

"Give me your hand, Ms. Jones." When she hesitated, he took her hand in his and turned it so her palm was face up. Taking a bit of the balm, he slipped it onto the inside of her wrist in lazy circular motions, feeling it heat up between their skin. Her eyes went just a little wide and her breath caught in her chest, making him want to massage the balm into her clit to see the sort of effect it would have on her. "What do you think?"

"It's hard to know for sure but...I think it could be quite...effective." She tried to pull her hand free of his, but he just pulled her closer...close enough that he could smell her perfume as it mingled with the citrusy herbal scent of the balm.

"Maybe we should explore its benefits further." Marshall caught her mouth in a kiss, tangling his fingers in her hair and pulling her to him as his tongue danced over hers, loving that she no longer seemed to be fighting what was between them.

Shifting them, he laid her back on the sofa, pinning her under his weight with his hips moving against hers so that his hard cock rode against her heat, his need for her casting out all other thoughts. Grabbing her hands, he lifted them up over her head and pinned them there, both her wrists held tight in one hand, so his other was free to wander, cupping her breasts and teasing her nipples. "Tell me you want this, Harper. Tell me that you want me to fuck you...that you want to feel my tongue on your clit, that you want my cock between your legs."

"I do. I want this so bad, Marshall. But..." He could feel her hesitation, and knew it had less to do with what was between them, and more about their situation.

He pulled back and kissed her, reining in how badly he wanted her, and then got to his feet, before pulling her up into his arms. "I think we should head out for the afternoon. Maybe continue our research at my place."

"Marshall...this is crazy. You know I'd like nothing more, but, you're my boss, you're in the middle of a divorce with a crazy woman who's having your baby, and I...well, I'm not in a great place either. We both have issues that make this a bad idea." She let out a weary sigh, but he couldn't bear the thought of letting her go.

"I'm taking you home with me, Harper. And we're going to work." He'd make sure of it. He'd also make sure they completed their research in a most thorough manner. "As for my ex, you're right—she is crazy. So if you're thinking that I'm somehow still hung up on her, you'd be mistaken. As for her being pregnant with my kid, well...I'll believe it when I see the DNA test—or a pregnancy test for that matter, since it could easily be just one more of her lies."

"Have you slept with her recently?" Harper cocked her head to the side, pinning him with a steely glare. "Because she didn't look pregnant to me, which means that if she is pregnant and it's yours, then it had to be fairly recent, right? And no offense, Marshall, but if you're still fucking her, then I'm not getting involved in your mess."

"Harper...I swear it's not like that. She came over about three-four months ago, really upset, and I felt bad for her—but I swear I don't remember sleeping with her." He knew how it sounded, especially if he had any hope of pursuing something with Harper. "I only had a glass of wine, and then...that was it. I woke up the next morning, and she was gone. It was odd, and I definitely felt off the next day, but I didn't give it much thought—until a few weeks ago when she announced she was pregnant."

"And you actually think I believe that?" She scoffed at him and turned to go when he grabbed her arm and pulled her to him.

"I swear it's the truth, Harper. I don't remember what happened." Which was more than a little odd, though he suspected that she'd drugged him.

She was still looking at him as if she didn't believe a word out of his mouth. "What'd she do? Roofie you?"

"Why does everyone keep asking me that?" He let out a weary sigh. "Though the truth of the matter is that yes...I do believe it was something along those lines, since I can't remember what happened, and that's totally out of character for me."

"Wow...that's really messed up, Marshall." Her brow furrowed and some of her anger turned to pity.

He cupped her cheek and kissed her sweetly. "It is, which

is why I can't dwell on it. Now grab your things, because we're getting out of here and heading to my place so I can fuck you until you don't remember anyone's name but mine."

It looked like she was going to argue with him, but in the end she packed up the toys and grabbed her handbag, pausing for a moment at the door. "Work first—and don't make me regret this, Marshall."

"You have my word, sunshine."

CHAPTER 6

Walking into Marshall's home, Harper had to admit that she was pretty damn impressed. Though the home was large, it still felt warm and welcoming, with plenty of natural materials throughout, from the stained wood beams overhead, to the stone details and soft leather furniture. It definitely felt like Marshall—classy, warm, and masculine. "This is really nice."

"I'm glad you like it." He slipped his arm around her waist and pulled her close, his muscular body hard against her soft curves. "After a long day, it's nice to have a place to retreat to that feels like home. When I was with Claire, I always felt like a guest in my own house. She had the place decked out like some ode to modern design. Everything was cold, hard, white and chrome. Made me crazy. I was happy to let her keep the loft when we split."

Somehow, Harper could see that, despite having met Claire for mere seconds. That woman didn't seem to have a warm and comforting bone in her body—which was in complete contrast to Marshall. How the two of them had ended up together, she hadn't a clue. And in a way, she was relieved to know that this wasn't the home he'd once shared with his wife. "Well, I think this place suits you perfectly—and it really is gorgeous. I guess that's one of the advantages of owning your own successful company."

"That and inheriting a good chunk of money. I sometimes wonder if that was Claire's original motivation." Marshall shrugged and seemed to shake it all off, as if Claire was of little significance, despite the problems she was causing him. He tipped her chin up and stole a kiss, his stubble rough against her skin as his lips lingered on hers, making her want so much more. "Get comfortable, Ms. Jones. I promised that we'd get work out of the way first, and I intend to do a most thorough job of seeing just how well the products work."

She wanted to argue that thoroughly researching the products would mean getting naked, and that he was clearly blurring the lines, but before she could say anything, he'd spun her around, and with a hard slap on her ass, had her moving across the room, the sting across her cheeks doing all sorts of other things to her. Scooping up the bags, he fell in by her side, his hand on the small of her back as he steered her towards his bedroom.

"You don't waste any time, do you?" She couldn't quite believe that they were actually going to do this. But as she looked up at him over her shoulder, she found him irresistible and damn sexy with his dark, mussed-up hair, warm brown eyes, and rough stubble. He was so tall—muscular too—and she had to admit, that she'd always been a sucker for a tall man, and had even more of a weak spot for intelligent men—which Marshall certainly was. Not that she ever indulged herself.

Well, today, that was clearly going to change, especially if Marshall had anything to say about it, since he already had his hands and mouth on her body as he moved them into his bedroom. He kissed her hard, his tongue darting past her lips as he gripped her hips in powerful hands, so she could feel the energy coursing through him just below the surface. It made her think of a feral beast, its body coiled tight in waiting as it stalked its prey, getting ready to take it down in a primal struggle.

Barely breaking away from his kisses, he tore the clothing from her body, his intensity spurring on her racing heart as she tried to maintain some semblance of control. And then she realized that it was pointless. She was no match for Marshall when he was determined, especially when he'd already stripped her naked, his hands possessive and his mouth hungry.

"You're fucking magnificent, Harper." Too impatient to wait for her to get around to undressing him, he made quick work of it himself, so that he now stood before her, naked, in all his powerful beauty. And he was beautiful...like some pagan sex god carved out of marble, his cock hard and long and absolutely perfect.

She told herself to snap out of it, to stop ogling him like she'd been on a year-long fast and he was a perfectly seared steak, even if it felt just like that. It'd been years since Josh, but...she couldn't think about him. Not now. Not when she was with Marshall.

So instead of coming to her senses, she dropped to her knees before him, her fingers around his hard length and her tongue lapping at the glistening jewel of pre-cum at the tip of his erect cock.

"Fuck, Harper..." The need in his ragged voice had her

wrapping her lips around his girth and eagerly sucking him, his fingers knotting in her hair and slowly thrusting into her mouth. "You look so fucking perfect with my cock in your mouth...I swear, it's doing me in."

She felt herself go wet, loving how he was taking charge, controlling the pace and how much of him she'd take, so it was all she could do not to come right then and there, her clit so swollen, it ached to be touched. As she moaned against his cock, desperately wanting all of him, he thrust into her mouth, giving her more with each pass as she stroked his shaft and his balls, feeling them tighten in her palm. Sensing how close he was, she sucked him harder, swirling her tongue around the head of his cock as she squeezed her legs together against the thrumming ache of her clit and the emptiness that begged to be filled, to be stretched tight around his hard length as he fucked her.

"Not yet, Ms. Jones." With a desperate groan, Marshall pulled his cock away, leaving her to protest, even as he lifted her to her feet and then scooped her up onto the bed, flipping her onto her hands and knees. "Don't move, or there'll be consequences."

And just to make sure she understood him, he slapped her ass, her pussy gushing in response as the flicker of red hot pain melted into the very essence of pleasure and need, leaving her desperate for more—and almost certainly guaranteeing that she'd be misbehaving. "Just so you know—this is a one-time deal, Marshall. So make sure you get everything out of your system and investigate all you want to investigate, because this thing between us is not happening again."

"Sunshine...you can't handle everything I have to give you—at least not yet—so I suggest you forget about issuing out demands when your ass is bare and sticking high in the air." The humor in his voice sounded so sexy, it nearly killed her. "Now let's see what Mistress Aria packed for us."

"Mistress?" She swallowed hard at the thought of all the extra items she may have thrown into their shopping bags.

"Did I not tell you? Must have slipped my mind." Except that she could tell he hadn't forgotten that little detail—not in the very least. "Looks like she anticipated our needs beautifully, Ms. Jones. Question is where to begin?"

"Aren't we supposed to be working?" She glared at him over her shoulder, only to find him kneeling on the bed, holding a pair of leather cuffs and a flogger. Her already racing heart skipped a few beats as she felt her wetness slip onto her thighs. But...what the hell...in for a penny, in for a pound. She might not have ever had an adventurous sex life before this, but she'd always been curious, even if she never thought to pursue it, and if she was going to actually sleep with her boss, then she might as well make it a night she'd never forget, since it'd likely be ages before she got laid again.

"We are working, Ms. Jones. I'm thinking of adding a secondary product line to help us expand beyond vibrators. And that means we should do a complete and thorough investigation of all there is to offer." Gently, he ran the flogger down along her spine, so she couldn't help but shimmy in response as the soft leather strands slipped down over her ass cheeks.

She found it nearly impossible not to moan and shift back towards him, desperate for more, for all he had to give her, even if she was giving him a hard time about it. "What if I'm not into that sort of thing? Did you ever think about that? Hmm?"

He gave her a teasing smile, slipping his fingers along her slick and swollen slit, and then brought his fingers to her lips so she could taste herself. "Are you really going to try to deny that you're not turned on by the thought of it? Though, by all means, if you want me to stop, just say so. I would never do anything to you that you didn't want...didn't truly enjoy. So tell me, Ms. Jones...would you like me to continue?"

Damn him. When she glared at him over her shoulder, there was no heat to it, knowing that at this point, she was in too deep to deny just how much she wanted him. "Might as well, since I already have my ass in the air."

The first lash fell hard, no doubt punishment for her sarcasm. And the sting was absolutely glorious, as was the touch of his hand afterwards as he gently soothed her skin, the gesture sweet and caring. "I find you very entertaining, sunshine."

She was still trying her best to resist him, though her tongue still had a mind all its own. "And you need to get on with it if we have any hope of finishing work tonight."

"Such a mouth on you..." The next lash fell quick and hard across her ass cheek, the sting blossoming into pleasure as she went so wet, she could feel it slipping onto her thighs. This time, when he brushed his fingers along her slit, he let them dip in, teasing her so she couldn't help but push back for more with a needy cry, desperate for his touch, desperate to have him fill her and make her come. "You're so wet...and so fucking tight. It really has been a long time for you, hasn't it?"

He was still thrusting his fingers in and out of her slowly, teasing her clit and slipping his fingers up to her ass before slipping back inside her, until she was biting back her moans. Gently, he let the soft leather of the flogger dance its way up her spine until her skin was electrified, breaking out in goose bumps as a wave of need slipped over her skin. "Come on, Marshall...don't be such a tease."

"That's the best part. Well...almost the best part. But if you think I'm going to rush through this when you've given me just one night, then you can guess again. I'm going to take full advantage of every moment I have with you." He pulled away and lashed her ass again—and this time the leather caught just enough of her pussy to make her ache for him desperately, her clit throbbing in desperation. "What is it you want, Ms. Jones?"

She groaned, knowing there was no avoiding it. "I want you to fuck me, Marshall."

"Oh, I will, sweet girl. But first let's see how this balm works when applied to something other than your wrist." It didn't take long for him to get out the small tin. A moment later, he was lazily circling his fingers around her clit and along her slick folds, dipping into her as a warmth tingled over her skin and a minty herbal scent filled the air.

The warmth turned into a heat that was at once searing hot and ice cold, sensitizing every nerve so that she was teetering on the verge of coming, his touch doing things to her that no one had ever done before. Her hips pushed back against his hand, searching him out, wanting him like she'd never wanted anyone else before, her focus now single-minded as her need for him obliterated any other thought. "Please, Marshall..."

"What do you think of the balm? 'Cause I have to say...you're even wetter now." Leaning over her with his broad chest pressed against her back, he kissed her cheek, his stubble rough against her skin, sending a shiver coursing through her. He reached into the drawer to grab a condom, even as her ass twitched and shimmied, searching him out, as his length nestled teasingly between her cheeks. "Patience, sunshine. I promise to take good care of you."

She needed to see him...needed to watch his magnificent form and his erect cock as he sheathed himself in latex. With each movement, she could see the muscles and tendons shift below his taut skin, his nimble fingers—the fingers of a surgeon—making quick work of it all. And then he was brushing the head of his cock against her slick opening, teasing her until she dropped her head to the mattress, her ass high in the air as if in offering.

It was then that she heard the quiet buzzing sound. He slipped the U-shaped couple's vibe inside her, the vibrations against her clit and G-spot nearly doing her in, since she was already riding that edge from him teasing her. All it took was for him to slide his cock inside her, his wide girth and generous length pushing her over the edge, so she came with that single thrust, his name on her lips as she cried out, her body quivering in its release.

And yet, they were only just beginning.

CHAPTER 7

"**S**weet girl...that** was so quick." Marshall knew he'd pushed Harper to the edge and had left her there, teetering precariously, so it took very little to finally send her over that cliff, especially with the vibe and his cock stretching her tight. "What do you think of the vibrations?"

"I think they need to stop or I'm going to come again." Her legs were all but trembling as her body braced against the building energy.

Gripping her hips tightly, he slowly pulled his cock out until just the head remained buried inside her, and then thrust back into her, forcing his full length into her sweet cunt. She was so slick and wet, and though the vibrations certainly heightened things for him, he also found the device a bit distracting, and not all that comfortable.

Her fingers fisted the comforter on his bed as he thrust into her, again and again, her needy moans refusing to be silenced even as she tried to bury them in the crook of her arm. This time, when he pulled back, he did so fully, though it was only long enough to remove the vibe, and bury himself once more. "That's better, don't you think?"

She nodded even as he thrust into her, taking her more fully and with greater ease now that the vibe wasn't in the way. Despite her gorgeous plump ass, it wasn't enough...he wanted more from her, especially when he was so close to coming, her tight body too delicious to not have him riding that edge.

He pulled out of her, ignoring her protests as he switched their positions, lying back so she could straddle him. "Come on, love. That's it. This time I want to see your face when I make you come."

She bit her lower lip as she eased herself down his thick shaft, bracing herself with her small hands on his chest, so he had the most perfect view of her. She was absolute perfection, with milky skin, dark mahogany hair that tumbled over her full breasts and tight nipples, with curvy hips that trailed to firm thighs and the sweetest cunt ever.

Her hips moved in an undulating rhythm up and down his cock as he thrust up into her, quickening their pace. Unable to resist, he sat up and caught her hard rosy nipple between his teeth and sucked it into his mouth with a firm arm around her waist so he could bury himself completely inside her, forcing her body to stretch around him, to take all of him as he claimed her, his head dizzy with how much he wanted her.

And then she was coming as he swallowed her cries with a kiss, his own release flooding through him as his cock pulsed deep inside her, already desperate to have her once again. They rode out the last tremors of their orgasm together, their heavy breathing now one as he continued to kiss her, until he was finally able to speak. "That was excellent work, Ms. Jones."

She bit his bottom lip and gave him an easy smile. "You

weren't so bad yourself, Dr. Foley."

***

Drowsy with sleep, Marshall reached over to pull Harper into his arms, desperately wanting her even if he'd spent half the night with her sweet body wrapped around his cock.

Except that the bed was empty, pulling him more fully from his slumber. There was no light on in the bathroom, and a quick glance at the time told him it was too early for her to be starting her day. Four seventeen in the morning. He forced himself to leave the warmth of his bed, and quickly realized that her clothes, tossed haphazardly on the floor the night before, were now gone.

"Fuck." His gut roiled and his chest tightened, irritated, and hurt. She'd fucking pulled a runner.

She'd said she'd give him one night, but he hadn't expected her to up and leave before the sun even dawned. He thought they'd had a good time—even thought he might be able to change her mind for a repeat performance, especially when he couldn't remember the last time he'd actually enjoyed himself and let go of all his problems.

Harper had somehow done that for him.

Except that she'd slunk out of his bed and home like a thief in the night. And he may have had plenty of years under his belt as a bachelor, and would likely have several more to come, but he'd never been so rude as to leave in the middle of the night without even a note or explanation. The fact that Harper had done just that pissed him off.

By the time he got into the office, he was in a foul mood, his temper up—which was a damn rare thing—and ready to hunt down Ms. Harper Jones. She wasn't in her office, nor was she waiting for him in his, though he immediately spotted the report on his desk. His eyes narrowed as his anger raced like poison in his veins. She'd fucking left his bed so she could type him up a complete and thorough report on all the products they'd used the night before.

If he wasn't so pissed off, he'd probably find it amusing. But he didn't. Not in the least bit. And where the fuck was she? Was she even at the office or had she dropped off the report and then left, knowing she'd have to face him?

And then, just because the universe wanted to completely fuck with him, Claire stormed into his office, already crying her crocodile tears. Before she could even park her ass in a chair, he grabbed her arm and started marching her back out and towards the elevators. "If you have anything at all to say to me, you tell your lawyer to speak to my lawyer. Or I will file a restraining order against you, and then laugh my ass off when they throw you in jail for violating it—which I know you'd do."

"You're such a mean fucking bastard, Marshall. All I wanted was to try to work things out between us. And now our baby..." She choked back a sob, and pouted at him as he hit the elevator button.

"Until I see DNA evidence, I don't believe that baby's mine—if you're even pregnant." The doors opened and he shoved her onto the elevator, hitting the down button before stepping off. "I'm calling the cops, so if you know what's good for you, you'll be gone before they get here."

With clenched fists, she stomped her feet like a two-year old having a tantrum. "I fucking hate you, Marshall."

"Believe me, the feeling's mutual." Before she could get another word in, the doors slid shut, though her absence did little to ease his anger with the world that morning. And where the fuck was his temp?

He stalked through the building, his pace brisk as his employees hurried out of his way with their morning cups of coffee, his eyes scanning the halls and offices for Harper.

There she was…at her old job, sitting at her desk, laughing and chatting with one of her coworkers—until she spotted him, the room going silent. "Ms. Jones…my office. Now—if you'd be so kind."

He didn't want to be an unreasonable ass, but he was fucking pissed off, and in no mood for niceties. Her coworker's eyes went a little wide as she looked from him to Harper as if wondering what the hell was going on, and Marshall knew without a doubt that the rumor mill would be churning like crazy. Not that he gave a rat's ass. Whatever was between him and Harper didn't concern anyone else.

Somehow he found the strength to refrain from touching her as they walked down the hall and through the building, though he wasn't sure he'd be able to keep his hands off her once they were behind closed doors. She was making him absolutely crazy.

Once in his office, she glared at him and paced the floor as he closed the door behind them. "I don't understand what this is about."

"What it's about is you leaving in the middle of the night and not having the courtesy to wake me up to let me know you're going or even bothering to leave me a note." He shook his head as if to clear it. "You get that it's not normal to go sneaking out of someone's house in the middle of the night. Right?"

"You mean it's not normal for a woman—'cause I do believe guys sneak out before morning all the time." She gave him a shrug as if to say that they both knew she was right.

"Maybe other guys would, but that's not me, and I guess I expected a bit of common courtesy, given the fact that I made you come so many times last night that I lost count." He tossed his hands up in the air, his frustration getting the better of him.

"And it was amazing. I honestly had a great time. But I'd told you it was just the one night." She let out a sigh and wrapped her arms around herself as if to ward off a chill. "I had...things I needed to take care of."

"Things? And those things couldn't wait another few hours until morning?" He half wondered if there'd been someone at home waiting for her... "Please do not fucking tell me you had to rush back to some boyfriend you didn't tell me about."

"The only one waiting for me was my cat—who, by the way, was none too happy with me. And just so we're clear— I'm not like that, Marshall. I don't lie, and I sure as hell don't cheat. So if you think I'm anything like your ex, I'll stop you right there. I'm loyal." Closing the distance between them, she reached over and gave his hand a squeeze, his heart finally easing a little. "I get that she's messed with your head, but...you clearly don't know me—even if we've slept together."

"That may very well be the case, but it doesn't have to stay that way." Needing to touch her, to feel her close, he cupped the back of her neck and pulled her to him, nuzzling her, her breath catching in response. His heart ached with the uncertainty between them, but in that moment, he swore he'd never wanted anyone more. "Fuck, Harper...I'd love to get to know you better. Hell, I've wanted nothing more since you started working here nine months ago, even if I tried to keep my distance. And this does not have to be anything complicated, but I'm not settling for just one night. It's not fucking happening. One night is nowhere near enough."

He didn't give her even a moment to think about it, nor a moment to protest, covering her mouth with a kiss and hauling her body to his, pinning her against his desk, taking, tasting, as his cock pressed against her heat. She softened against him, kissing him back as he lifted her onto his desk, her legs wrapping around his thighs and her hips grinding against his cock.

Fucking hell, he was ready to take her right then and there on his desk in the middle of the workday—until she broke off their kiss, though she didn't pull away, lingering in his arms. "We can't do this, Marshall. You're my boss."

"Did you sleep with me because I'm your boss?" He didn't think so, but since they were discussing it, he might as well find out.

She rolled her eyes at him and let out an exasperated sigh. "I slept with you because you're smoking hot, smart, and you turn me on. Though to be fair, some of that probably has to do with the fact that my sex life has been nonexistent. And if I do decide to sleep with you again, it still won't be because you're my boss—it'll be because you have a magnificent cock and you know how to use it. Not that I'm saying I'm going to sleep with you again."

Yet to Marshall, it sounded an awful lot like she was going to do just that. With her words rattling around in his head, he gave her a smile, some of the tension in his chest finally easing. "No...of course not, Ms. Jones."

CHAPTER 8

Harper **double-checked that** she had her passport packed in her handbag, still not quite believing she'd be off to London in just a few hours. She must be insane. And though she'd emailed her brother, Brian, to let him know she'd be gone, she still wanted to make sure he wouldn't forget, especially since he hadn't even bothered to write back. "Like I said, I'll be gone on a business trip, so just make sure you check in on Dad. I did his grocery shopping for him, but you know how he gets if left alone for too long."

Harper checked in on her dad nearly every day, and was worried about leaving him to go away with Marshall to this conference. Her mom's death several years ago had left her dad in a funk, and losing himself in a bottle of whiskey seldom made his depression better. She'd tried to get him help, but her mom had been his everything, and he was lost without her.

"Yeah...I suppose I can manage it since it's just a week, though...Harper...he's a grown man. He can take care of himself." Brian sounded frustrated, but she didn't care. She seldom asked for his help.

The only other people she could depend on were her twin cousins, Archer and Hawke, who were dear friends of hers. The truth was, she'd always felt closer to them than her own brother, even if she didn't see them as often as she'd like.

She knew they'd do anything they could to help her, but they lived out of the way on a small island in Maine, and it would be a haul for them, when her brother was just a few towns over. They'd even offered to get her dad into a rehab place that would not only address his addiction but his depression, though expensive as it was, she was trying to avoid taking their money, hoping to save enough to pay for it herself.

"He might be a grown man, but we've seen how well he's managed in the past when left to his own devices. So unless you can convince him to get some real help, I need you to check in on him. It's only a damn week, Brian." It's not as though she wasn't also frustrated, but she couldn't just abandon her father, even if he refused to do anything about his situation.

"I'll see you when you get back then. Have a good time, Harper—and try not to work too hard."

"I'll try not to." Relieved that her dad would be taken care of, she finished packing, left instructions for the pet sitter, and gave her cat one last hug, knowing Marshall would be there to pick her up at any moment. Working by his side the last few days while trying to resist him had been close to impossible—and yet she'd managed to focus on work, even if her body kept trying to talk her into just one more night in his arms, one more night as he claimed her time and again.

With her coworkers around, and the rumors already flying, it'd been just enough to get her to hold her ground and resist him. But a week away in London with just the two of them? She didn't know if she could be that strong. Not when the mere sight of him walking into a room was enough to have her heart leaping inside her chest—among other things.

By the time Marshall knocked on her door, her nerves were getting the better of her, not just because she was always a hot mess when she had to fly, but because she was going away with him, and she knew the rules were about to change. It didn't help that she still didn't know what the hell they were doing. Part of her knew it could be a huge mistake to sleep with him again, especially when she was growing more attached to him with each passing day. But another part of her would happily jump into his bed in a heartbeat since sex with Marshall was amazing and unlike anything she'd experienced before.

She opened the door and found him standing there, looking heart-stoppingly gorgeous in jeans, a cranberry tee, and a worn leather jacket to ward off the chill of the brisk spring day. He leaned in and kissed her cheek like they were old friends, filling her head with his masculine scent. "Are you ready, sunshine?"

Something about having him so close sent her into a near panic, making her second-guess going on this trip. Because one thing was certain—she now knew she'd never be able to resist him for a whole week, her resolve already weakening. "I am, but...I don't know. Maybe you should go without me. I don't do so well on planes, and just think of all the work I could get done without you around to distract me and drag me off to breakfast."

His brows perked up as if not quite believing she was going to go down this road. "Harper...I need you with me. And this conference is exactly what we need for inspiration. It'll help us narrow down what direction to take our next product line in, and at this point...you're my muse and I need you by my side. If you're scared of flying, I promise to do all I can to distract you."

She let out the breath she didn't realize she'd been holding and glared at him. "That's what I'm afraid of, Marshall. I know the sort of distraction you're talking about and I'm telling you right now—I'm not sleeping with you again. I can't. So if that's what you're thinking is going to happen, then you can guess again. Am I clear?"

"What's clear, my sweet girl, is that I'm going to thoroughly enjoy myself during this trip."

***

Harper tried to slow her breathing as Marshall's private jet taxied the runway and the engines revved in preparation for taking off. Although this was a far cry from Josh's little plane, she still couldn't help the panic she felt inside, her pain and heartache coming to life once more. This might be a larger plane than the one Josh had been in when he crashed, but it could still fall out of the sky all the same. "I hate this part, Marshall. I never should have come with you. There was no need for it."

"Look at me, Harper." Marshall shifted in his seat and brushed her cheek, his brow furrowed with worry as her eyes burned with threatening tears. "It'll be okay, love...you have my word. I won't let anything happen to you."

"Some things aren't in your control." She sounded as

panicked as she felt, but then he was kissing her, slow and sweet, forcing her to focus on him, so that her fears and worries faded in his kisses.

He was making it so she could think of nothing but him, the memories of the time she spent naked in his arms playing out in her head. Her body craved him, ached for his touch, and left her desperately wanting him to take her again, even if she knew it would only complicate things further.

His tongue found hers as his kiss deepened, her fingers gripping the soft cotton of his tee as she held onto him. And though his kisses eventually slowed, he continued to hold her close, cradling her to him and enveloping her in the safety of his arms. "There you go, sweet girl... That wasn't so bad, right? We're up."

And so they were. She let out a ragged breath, and though she knew she should sit back in her own seat, instead she nestled in deeper in his arms. "I know I shouldn't be doing this—and I don't want you reading more into it than what it actually is, which is me just being stupidly chicken shit about flying. But you're warm and muscular, and you feel safe and smell good."

"Whatever you need, I'm here for you, Harper. I mean it." He ran his hand down her hair and kissed the top of her head as she settled deeper into his embrace, his steady and strong heartbeat soothing her.

A ragged breath escaped her lungs as the tension in her muscles slowly slipped free. "I don't know your ex at all, Marshall, but...man, she must be an idiot to mess things up with you."

He let out a small laugh and leaned his cheek against her

head. "So then why do you keep fighting what's between us, instead of giving in to it? Because there's definitely something there, Harper—even if it's nothing more than a bit of fun. You can't deny it."

She sat up out of his arms, just enough to be able to look up at him. "I'm not denying it—but you're also my boss, you're in the middle of a nasty divorce with a woman who's a bitch, which means you're likely on the rebound. And that's not even counting all of my issues." How could she let Josh go when he was still suffering, confined to a wheelchair, the pain unbearable? She already felt guilty enough about sleeping with Marshall. "Trust me when I tell you, I'm not a good bet either."

"Harper...are you looking for something serious? Because those issues only matter if you are—and that would be fine if that's what you need at this point in your life. I get that." He brushed her cheek with his thumb, his touch gentle and his eyes kind. "But if you're not, then why not enjoy ourselves? I can't remember the last time I had such a fun night—and I really like you...in case you hadn't noticed."

She couldn't help but smile. "Believe it or not, I did actually notice."

Everything he'd said was true. All their issues only mattered if there was more to their relationship than sex. And at this point, she didn't think she was capable of giving her heart to anyone, even if her body was desperate for some attention. And that meant that this thing with Marshall could be perfect.

Yet, something told her she'd be playing a dangerous game, and she knew, as sweet and sexy and smart as Marshall was, she could easily end up with a confusing mess on her hands. And that was a problem, which certainly meant all those other issues suddenly became major concerns.

"What's going on in that pretty head of yours, sunshine?" His thumb brushed her lips, making her breath catch and her heart race. She'd always found it such an erotic thing...as if he was claiming her mouth as his, as if he was reminding her of the things that mouth had done.

Yet she couldn't tell him what she was thinking, couldn't tell him that it'd be so easy to want more between them, so easy to fall for him. It was ridiculous to even go down that road when she was still so broken over Josh, and she and Marshall had only just started this thing between them. But she found herself suddenly wanting so much more for her life.

Josh had pushed her away, wanted no one around so he could mourn the life he'd once had—and she was nothing but a reminder of all he'd lost. But those three years alone to mourn her relationship with Josh had taken their toll, and now...Marshall had reminded her that she had a life to live.

But falling for him would be stupid when he was in no position to let this be anything but casual sex. And one thing was quickly becoming clear—she hadn't really ever been a casual kind of girl when it came to matters of the heart, and that seemed to be holding true when it came to Marshall. Not to mention the tiny little fact that he was her boss.

"What's going on in my head is that this is still a bad idea. I've worked too damn hard to build my reputation as an engineer who knows her shit, just to have it all ruined because I'm sleeping with the boss." There might be more to it than what she was saying, but it was still true. She knew the rumors were already flying around the company...and

85

she'd seen the looks they were giving her. Even Todd was looking at her like she'd stolen a position he was entitled to—and she'd always had a great working relationship with him. "People are already whispering to one another and looking at me like I'm the Whore of Babylon, especially after you promoted me to a position half of them would murder for, when I haven't even been with Clio a year. They think I'm trying to sleep my way to the top—and let's face it, that's exactly what it looks like from the outside looking in."

His brow furrowed with anger and his eyes blazed fierce. "That was my decision, and mine alone, Harper. You've more than proved yourself and your skills on other projects, not to mention your latest design. So if anyone gives you any problems, you tell me. Am I clear?"

She loved that he was so protective of her, but she knew that having him fight her battles would only make things worse. "No one's said anything to my face, but you know what it's like—and the last thing I need is for you to come to my defense. But...it's why this thing between us is a mistake." Among other things.

"It's one thing for you to not be interested in me, but if you're saying no because you're worried about what other people are going to say, then that's not fucking acceptable." He shook his head, and let out a deep breath between clenched teeth. "And you should know better than to let other people dictate how you live your life."

"This is my career, Marshall. What the hell am I supposed to do when you lose interest? Just go back to my cubby and pretend that nothing happened? How the hell can I even continue to work for Clio?" She knew he understood the problem, but was just choosing to ignore the reality, because he wanted to continue what they'd started.

"You can—and you will, Harper. People know you're good at what you do, and what you do in your personal life doesn't change that." He let out a frustrated sigh and stole another kiss, his lips lingering on hers. "I know this isn't easy for you, but fuck...it's been days since you were in my bed, and I haven't been able to think about anything else. That one night wasn't anywhere near enough."

"Well, it's going to have to be. You knew from the start that it was only a one-time thing." If she gave in, she'd only want more—a lot more than he was currently able to give her. And she knew that would be the case because the truth of the matter was that the mere thought of him sent her heart tripping over itself, and their night together had been running on an endless loop in her head, no matter how hard she tried to push it out of her head.

"I want this one week with you, Harper. Just you and me, naked in my bed, and I'm not taking no for an answer. I know you want this as bad as I do, so I'm not going to let you talk yourself out of it." His eyes blazed with a determination that sent her pulse skittering straight through to her core. "There won't be anyone else from Clio at this conference, and then once we get back, I promise not to ask you for anything more if you decide you want to put an end to it."

"Marshall...I can't." A week in his bed would guarantee her nothing but a world of trouble and heartache when she was already so close to falling for him. It'd be one thing if they'd just met, but they hadn't—she'd had nine months to develop feelings for him, feelings that were now amplified by the dangerous little game they were playing.

"You can and you will, Ms. Jones. Because I'm not taking no for an answer."

CHAPTER 9

Marshall swore Harper was making it so he couldn't think straight. What had started as a bit of a fun distraction with a gorgeous and smart woman was quickly becoming a need that refused to be extinguished or ignored. And though she hadn't agreed to give him this week together, he was a determined man.

Not having her again just wasn't an option.

Maybe Claire had left him completely fucked up. But he was starting to think that his need for Harper had absolutely nothing to do with his other problems. Because it was clear that there was more to it than her simply being a distraction from his divorce and the trouble Claire was stirring up.

Harper stifled a scream as the plane took a dip and shook as they hit some turbulence. With her still in his arms, he held her tightly to him. "It's okay, love. It's just a bit of bad weather. It'll pass."

"I know..." She took a deep breath, though she was so tense, he swore she'd be sore for days if he couldn't get her to relax. "It's silly, but...I just had a bad experience, I guess."

"It's not silly. Everyone has issues from their past that

they have to deal with." Just like he had to deal with the fact that he always had to be the best, because no matter what he did, his father always saw his kids as disappointments, as not good enough, and had no problem voicing his feelings on the matter. "Which is exactly why you should let me distract you, Harper."

She sat up out of his arms and ran her hands down her face, looking exasperated. "I can't give you a week, Marshall...things between us are already so complicated—at least it feels that way on my end. And a week with you would only leave my life even more messed up than it already it is."

"Harper...I know I don't know you well at all, but if you have issues you're dealing with and I can somehow help, then I'm happy to." He had more money than he'd ever be able to spend, and if her problems were money-related, then he'd do whatever he could to take care of the matter for her.

"It's just...personal stuff. And it's nothing I want to talk about. Besides, you have enough problems of your own with your ex wreaking havoc and making your life miserable." She chewed her bottom lip, her grey eyes darkening. "Were you at least happy at one point?"

Marshall wasn't quite sure how she'd turned things around on him, but he supposed that if he wanted her to open up to him, then he needed to do the same. "I was—or at least I thought I was. But the truth is that I don't think she ever loved me, and the person I fell in love with didn't ever really exist. It was all an act. I was never anything but a meal ticket to her, and I don't think there was ever a time in our relationship when she wasn't cheating on me."

And yet, despite having his heart betrayed, he was still

looking for happiness.

"You deserved better than that, Marshall." She slipped her hand into his, and nestled in against his side. "I've never understood people like that. It's so hard to find happiness. You'd think that once you have it in your grasp, you'd do all you could to hold onto it."

"I suppose she wasn't ever happy—though I doubt she was really looking for happiness anyway. I was just too stupid not to see it." It was the one and only time he'd fallen for someone's lies. Never again, though. "It's why you don't have to worry about this becoming serious, Harper. I know you're worried about that—but you don't need to be. I'll admit that I want you something fierce, but it's just a hunger that's looking to be fed. I'm not looking for anything more from you—especially if you're also not looking for anything serious."

"I'm not, Marshall. But..." She took a huge breath and let it out with a shake of her head. "But you're sexy, and charming, and you're really sweet, and that can be a dangerous combination. It's been awhile since I was...involved with anyone seriously. And I'm not looking for any sort of relationship, but...it doesn't mean that I don't run the risk of falling for you if I give in to what you're asking for. And that's not a chance I'm willing to take. This trip needs to be about work. Nothing more."

"It's just one week, Harper. I swear, I can almost guarantee I'll manage to be a big enough jerk and push your buttons enough to make sure you're happy to be rid of me." He bit her lip, doing all he could to hold himself back and not drag her into the private suite at the back of the plane. "One week, Ms. Jones. I'm a determined man. And then we can both go back to denying the attraction between us."

She all but groaned in frustration as she tried to push him away. "I can't, Marshall. I'm sorry, but there's no way this will work, even if it is just a week. And when we get back from the conference, I want my old job back."

"And I want you as my assistant—as my muse—and I won't take no for an answer." No fucking way. Why did it suddenly feel like instead of things moving forward between them, they were instead moving back? But if it was about work, then that's what he'd try to appeal to. "I'm offering you an amazing opportunity, Harper. You'd be able to pick and choose the projects you want to work on, help me decide the direction to take our product lines in."

"But not because I've put my time in with the company and proved myself, but rather because you want to fuck me." She let out a groan of frustration. "Don't you see the problem?"

"What I see is an engineer who came to me with an amazing idea, and probably has plenty more ideas where that one came from. No one else has done that. No one else has taken the initiative to develop a project they weren't assigned to and has come up with something that's completely out of the box." Didn't she see how incredible she was? What an asset she could be? "I'm not saying I don't want to fuck you, Harper—because clearly I do. Once was nowhere near enough. But that doesn't mean that you're not remarkable at your job and that you'd be a bigger asset to Clio if you were working with me on innovating our products."

"I'm grateful for the opportunity, Marshall, but..." Her shoulders slumped as she wrapped her arms around herself. "I'm still not sure I'm the right person for that particular job."

He couldn't believe he was going to voice his suspicions about the mole, but he had to get her to see just what was at stake. "What if I told you there was more to it? What if I told you that I needed someone I could trust with the innovations we'd be working on, because I suspect someone is leaking information to our competitors?"

"You can't be serious, Marshall. Really?" Her eyes went wide and then she slowly shook her head to clear it. "Who would do such a thing?"

"I wish I knew. But it's why I need to try to figure out what's happening. If I can take control of where we take our product lines, and limit who comes in contact with the designs until we're ready for production, I can try to contain this." The problem was he had no real proof—just one too many design similarities. It had gone from feeling like bad luck to something that occurred too frequently to be simple coincidence.

"So...not to put me under a magnifying glass, but...how do you know you can trust me?" When she chewed her lip, he couldn't help but steal a kiss.

"The truth is I don't know that I can trust you—even though I do." Before Claire, he'd thought himself a pretty good judge of character. He swore Harper wouldn't betray him, even though a part of him—the part of him that had gotten burned by a cheating, lying spouse—left him questioning how trustworthy anyone really was, when there were few people who didn't have a price. "That said, if there's just the two of us working on a design, and it shows up elsewhere, then at the very least we've narrowed the field considerably."

"I don't know if I want that sort of responsibility, Marshall. And no offense, but I don't know what lengths your competitors will go to for that sort of information. I know we're not exactly dealing with world-changing technology, or nuclear weapons and such, but there's a lot of money to be made in this industry, and...people get greedy." She let out a deep breath and shifted her gaze, refusing to let it settle on him for too long. "And that's all the more reason why I can't sleep with you again, Marshall."

"One has nothing to do with the other, Ms. Jones—and this discussion isn't over. Like I've said before—I'm a determined man."

***

It was late by the time they got to the hotel in London, but their suite was perfect, though he wondered just how smart it was to stay in the hotel the conference was actually being held in. It was already bustling with people, though the conference didn't start for another day, with tomorrow being a soft open, allowing the vendors to get set up while people continued to fly in.

"Why is there only one bed?" Harper spun on him and pinned him with a glare as he tipped the porter and locked the door.

"There's only one bed because originally I was going to be the only one coming to this event." Granted, he probably could have found a way to change it afterwards, but it wouldn't have been easy. "With the hotel already fully booked for the conference, I figured it'd be easier for me to sleep on the pullout sofa if it came to that."

"If it came to that? You're unbelievable." With a hand on her hip, she shook her head, her eyes narrowing as he closed the distance between them. "This is not going to work."

"Well, it's going to have to, since there aren't any other rooms available." If he only had a week with her, then he was going to make the most of it, even if they were there for work. "I promise to behave myself. Cross my heart and hope—"

"Don't say it, Marshall." He swore the color drained from her face, making him wonder if there was more to it than just keeping him out of her bed.

"Hey..." Concerned, he crossed to her side and ran a hand down her arm, hoping to reassure her. "The sofa should be a pullout, okay? I'll sleep there."

She nodded though her gaze refused to meet his. And then she was stepping away from him to get her suitcase. "Do we have a set schedule of when and where we need to be? And will we be manning a booth or table?"

"We use a distributor in Europe, and they'll be the ones highlighting our products at the show and manning the booth. I do have a panel I'm speaking on in a few days, but I'm here primarily to get a feel for upcoming trends." He couldn't tell if she was worried about something or just upset, but it was making him crazy to see her upset. And as skittish as she was looking, he didn't want to push her, suspecting that if he didn't give her a bit of space, he'd kill any chance he had to make things work between them, professionally and otherwise. "Why don't we go grab some dinner and then we can go over the schedule once we get back? There's a party we might have to hit too, since our distributor is the one hosting it."

She looked a little nervous at the prospect of going to the party—and she was probably right to think it was going to be pretty risqué. But she managed a brave smile anyway. "Sounds good."

Instead of ordering takeout or heading to some fancy restaurant with pretentious food, they ended up at this mom-and-pop Indian place that Marshall had been to on some previous visits to London. "I know it's a bit of a hole-in-the-wall, but I swear this place has some of the tastiest curries I've ever eaten."

She took a few bites of the different dishes she spooned onto her plate, and gave him a look of ecstasy. "This is really amazing, Marshall. Thanks for bringing me along, even though I fought you every step of the way."

"I'd happily do it all again. Believe me. I hate coming to these things alone." He helped himself to some more lamb Vindaloo and fragrant basmati rice.

"So, what else is scheduled for the week? Anything in particular you want to accomplish?" Clearly she was determined to keep him focused on work. And that was fine. The night was still young, there was only one bed in their room, and he still had the whole week ahead of him, if she needed more time.

"I just want us to get inspired...get a feel for where the market and our competitors are headed. There might be some panels worth sitting in on, and other than that, there are a few parties we've been invited to. I'd prefer to give them a miss, but I need to, at the very least, make an appearance." Most of the parties would likely be too extreme and crazy for Harper, but there were still a few he'd need to attend.

"I can just imagine the sort of parties that happen at these sorts of conventions." Of course, she was right, especially since the convention wasn't just sex toys, but everything sex related, from BDSM equipment to adult movies and entertainment.

"Honestly, I don't think your imagination could dream up half the stuff that goes on at these things, and frankly I think it's best kept that way." She was already so standoffish, and he didn't want to push her over the edge with the sort of things that bore no relevance to his life or business.

"I'm not some prude, Marshall." She gave him an annoyed glare. "And my motto's always been 'to each their own.' I don't judge people for what turns them on as long as everyone involved has fully consented to the activities. So don't go assuming I'm some sort of close-minded and sheltered nun who needs her virtue and purity protected."

He barked out a laugh and gave her a sly smile. "Fair enough. Does that mean you'll share the bed with me tonight?"

She shook her head with a smile. "I swear, you have a one-track mind."

"When it comes to getting you naked? Damn right, I do."

CHAPTER 10

Harper took another bite of her curry, not quite sure how she'd get Marshall—and herself—to behave themselves once they got back to the hotel. She hadn't been able to stop thinking about their one night together, which immediately sent a shiver of need through her body, reminding her that she had a whole lot of time to make up for when it came to her lack of a sex life.

"I'll have to get changed before we go to this party, although...I just hope I have something appropriate. I'm not exactly sure what the dress code will be at these sorts of things." She could just imagine what it'd be like.

Reaching across the table, Marshall ran a finger over the back of her hand, his touch lingering before he slipped her hand into his. "Sweetness, no matter what you wear, you'll look smoking hot—and that's all you need to be for these sort of parties."

"And what about work? Anything I need to focus on while we're there?" She had to keep reminding herself that she was there to work—not to have sex with her boss. Or at the very least, not to just have sex with her boss.

"Just be your charming self, and have a good time. I'll take care of everything else." Why the hell did everything he say sound so damn sexy? Or maybe it was her, and being around Marshall had permanently put her mind in the gutter.

Knowing she was heading down a road that would only lead to the two of them getting naked, she forced herself to focus on work—and the biggest problem he'd mentioned thus far. "So the competition...they have some of our designs? Are you sure?"

"Pretty sure, unfortunately. But I think that we can stay ahead of the competition, especially now that we'll be pursuing your design for delivering deeper vibrations." He ran a rough hand across his stubbled chin as if in thought. "Have you shown your designs to anyone but Todd?"

She had to give it some thought, wondering if she'd mentioned it to anyone in her department. "No. I don't think I have, though that's not to say that my work wasn't ever left unattended at my desk. Until now, there's been no reason to be careful about locking away our work. But...damn, Marshall. I still can't believe someone at Clio is actually betraying us."

It was such an amazing company to work for. She couldn't believe someone would go to such lengths. She had to wonder who it might be. There were too many people who could easily access the designs they were working on.

"We'll figure it out, but that's why it'll be just the two of us for these upcoming projects. Hopefully by the time we're ready for production, we'll have figured out who the mole is." With their hands still linked, he brushed his thumb over the back of her hand, his smile making her heart race as her body came alive, making her fully aware of the effect he could have on her, even with a simple touch. "And in the meantime, I'm going to make sure you have everything you need at your disposal to bring your designs to life. Whatever you need, you just let me know."

She knew her design was a good idea, but too often, ideas got scrapped because they might be too costly, especially when it came to production, and reconfiguring the manufacturing. The fact that Marshall was willing to give her the chance to perfect her design and technology was huge. But something nagged at her, making her doubt his motivations. "Tell me this isn't just because you want to sleep with me."

Giving her hand a squeeze, he shook his head no. "Harper...it's a brilliant design. Don't you dare question it just because I'm going to fuck you until your knees go weak. Our competition would kill to get their hands on this sort of technology. And we'll patent it, of course—with your name on the design so you get a percentage of the profits."

His generous offer had her forgetting about the little fact that he'd just told her he was going to fuck her again.

"Really?" She'd been working for Clio when she developed the design, and most companies wouldn't have given her that sort of credit nor would they allow her to profit from it, having signed all sorts of non-competes and disclosure forms. This would give her the right to a percentage of the income, even though she'd have been happy just to be given the credit. "Marshall...that's really generous of you."

"You went above and beyond the scope of your job, Harper, so it's only fair that you reap some of the rewards." His fingers teased a path over the delicate skin on the inside of her arm, forcing her to press her legs together to try to keep her clit from throbbing.

"Well..." Bloody hell, she sounded breathless. "I truly appreciate it." The money would go a long way to getting her father the help he needed—if she could get him to agree to go.

He must have caught a glimpse of something in her eyes, because he suddenly looked concerned about her. "Harper, if there's anything at all that you need...if you need money or help... It's just that I've seen glimpses of worry and hurt in your eyes, and it's killing me. I'd love to help you if I can."

"And that's awfully sweet of you, but...I'll manage." The last thing she wanted was to involve him in her messy life.

"Will you really?" He clearly didn't believe her. Not that it mattered.

"Don't you have enough of your own problems to deal with?" She pulled her hand away from his and played with the food on her plate, her good mood evaporating though she knew she'd been short with him when he was just worried about her. "Look, Marshall...I appreciate your offer to help, but...my problems are my own. And frankly, I'm not looking to be reminded of them."

"Except that you know my problems. Everyone does. Yet you haven't told me a single thing about you, even though I only want to help." He sat back, frustration tensing his body so that it was clear he was now wound tight.

Feeling like a jerk for pushing him away, she reached over and gave his hand a squeeze. "I suppose being a doctor and all, you always want to help...always want to fix things."

"If I can, then why not?" He twined his fingers with hers, the tension in him now gone as he pinned her to the spot with his charismatic gaze and sexy smile. "I know you want to push me away, but I'm not going to let you."

The way he looked at her, the determination in his voice, left her body thrumming with need, her clit swollen and aching to be stroked by his strong fingers and his stiff tongue. She squeezed her legs together as she went wet, desperate for some relief, and fully aware that Marshall could easily give her what she needed.

A knowing smile slipped onto his lips, his eyes glinting in the glow of the soft restaurant lights. "You're thinking of me fucking you. Aren't you, Ms. Jones?"

She felt her cheeks flame, even as she denied the truth. "I have more important things to think about, Marshall."

"Like what?" His tone was so matter-of-fact, and the thought of having to answer his question left her squirming in her seat, knowing she'd been caught in a lie. "Because I do believe you're lying to me, sunshine—and if that's the case, then I do believe you've been rather naughty and might need to be punished."

She huffed in exasperation, wondering how he always managed to leave her so turned on and frustrated at the same time. "Fine. I lied. I was picturing you with your head between my legs, licking my cunt. Is that what you want to hear?" She ignored the wide-eyed looks the woman at the table next to them was giving her, her fork paused halfway to her mouth.

"I suppose it's a start." He picked up his glass of wine and took a sip, though his eyes remained locked on hers. "What else would you like me to do to you, Ms. Jones?"

She wanted to cringe...not just because he could feel her blush travel all the way down her neck to her chest, but because her nipples had gone hard, and her pulse was now echoing as a needy beat in her swollen clit. "I'm not having this conversation with you. Not here, not now."

"As you wish, love, since we still have that party to get to. But this conversation is far from over...and there will be consequences for your disobedience."

She should be appalled...and yet she'd never been so turned on in all her life.

Damn it.

CHAPTER 11

Marshall didn't know what had gotten into him, but one thing was sure: he was going to thoroughly enjoy himself—and if he only had a week alone with Harper, then he was going to make the most of every moment they had together.

"Just because we have to head out to this party doesn't mean I'm not going to have fun teasing you—especially since you're downright stunning." She looked gorgeous in a slinky little black dress with a plunging back that all but guaranteed he wouldn't be able to keep his hands off her.

Pulling her close, he nuzzled her, loving how she went soft in his arms, her breath catching in her chest. And then he was kissing her, like she was the only thing that could sustain him. His tongue clashed with hers as she fisted her fingers in his shirt, and the fact that she clearly wanted him as bad as he wanted her made him want to tear her dress from her body so he could feast on her.

Knowing he was too close to losing all semblance of control, he forced himself to break away from their kiss, though he still held her close. Letting his hands skim over her thighs, he caught the hem of her dress and he lifted it high enough to hook the edge of her lace panties. "These here? I hate to tell you, sunshine, but they're not coming with us."

"Marshall...what the hell are you doing?" The way she blushed and bit her bottom lip only made him want her all the more, his self-control tenuous at best.

"Hush, sunshine." Kneeling down before her, he slipped the panties down past her hips and plump ass, his hands lingering over her skin as he pulled them down, her hand on his shoulder to steady herself as he helped her step out of them. He stuffed them into the pocket of his dark jeans, and then, unable to resist, he pressed his lips to her soft skin and trailed kisses up her thighs before nudging them apart just a little so he could run his tongue against her slick folds. "You're so fucking wet and ready for me. Aren't you, love?"

Her breath caught as he flicked her clit with his tongue, her teeth sinking into her bottom lip as she tangled her fingers in his hair. "What would you do if I said no?"

"I'd call you a liar." He pulled the small vibrating plug from where he'd stashed it in his pocket while she was getting dressed, and slipped it against her slick lips before applying just enough pressure to ease it inside her, slowly teasing her clit before forcing himself to pull away. He hadn't turned it on yet, but there was plenty of time for that, and since it was one of his products, he knew the vibrations would not only be discreet, but powerful.

When Marshall got to his feet and let the fabric of her dress slip back down over her thighs, she frowned at him. "You can't expect me to go out like this. This dress is way too short to be running around without any panties on."

"I do expect it, and you will, Ms. Jones. Unless you want a butt plug to join the vibe." He gave her a stern look, knowing that she liked it when he was in control. "Or perhaps you'd like your ass paddled to keep it warm now that it'll be bare."

"You're a pain in the ass, Marshall." She glared at him, though there was no heat in her eyes. And when he pulled her close with a firm arm around her waist, her body softened against his, her breath catching as he bent his head to hers so he could bite her lip.

"Sweetness, if that's what you really want, I'm happy to oblige you—after we've returned from the party." Marshall knew that by waiting until they got back, especially when they'd be teasing each other through the night, would only intensify every touch, every sensation, when he did finally have her. "Not that we'll be staying long if I can help it."

She gave him a scolding look that made him want to put her over his knee and spank her ass red. "I'm not quite sure how you've managed to get me to ignore the little fact that we're supposed to keep things purely professional."

"It's just one of my many talents when it comes to you and you alone, Ms. Harper Jones. But just so we're clear, I don't believe I ever said anything contrary to the effect that I wanted nothing more than to fuck you until you were screaming my name." He brushed her cheek and stole a kiss, his lips lingering on hers. "Now let's get to that party before I decide it'll be more fun to turn on that vibe and see how many times we can get you to come."

The party was being held at a local club by his European distributor, and was already thronged with people by the time they got there. Clio might be a relatively small company, but they'd captured a good portion of the market with their constant innovations. The head of the sales and marketing department at their distributor waved Marshall down, stepping away from the small group he was with to welcome them.

"Klaus...good to see you again." Most of their business was conducted via phone or email, though they'd met on a few occasions. Marshall made sure to speak loud enough to be heard over the thumping bass of the music, which thankfully wasn't so loud that one couldn't carry on a conversation. "This is one of my most brilliant engineers, Harper Jones. Harper, this is Klaus Geisler from Oaken Inc."

"It's a pleasure." Klaus shook Harper's hand, his touch lingering as his gaze took her and he gave her a dashing smile, all sparkle and charisma. "Beauty and brains...the best of combinations. Will you be in London long?"

"Just for the conference. I'm afraid I've left several projects on hold, and I'm eager to get back to them." When she glanced over at Marshall, he shifted closer to her so that her body brushed against his. And as his head filled with her fruity scent, he couldn't help but slip his arm around her waist, not only because he desperately wanted her, but because he also wanted to make sure Klaus understood that she was taken.

"Well, I've no doubt Marshall will remind you to balance work with pleasure." Klaus gave Marshall a sly look as if telling him he was a lucky bastard—which he most certainly was, since Marshall was going to be the one fucking Harper later that night. "Make sure you see me before you go. And tonight is fun only. Have a great time, and we'll catch up on work later."

As Klaus wandered away, Marshall tightened his hold on Harper and pulled her to him, catching her mouth in a kiss as her curves slipped against his hard-on. He caught the lobe of her ear between his teeth and ran his hands down to her ass, cupping her cheeks in his palms. "Did you see how much Klaus wanted you? But you're all mine, sunshine."

"Am I now?" When she looked up at him with a mischievous smile and started to slip away, he grabbed her hand and pulled her to him once more, tightening his hold on her as he shifted them back into a shadow.

"You most certainly are, Ms. Jones." And then, as if to prove his point, he fingered the remote to the vibe and flicked it on, pleased to see her eyes go wide. "However, I'm happy to remind you if need be."

"Marshall..." Her hands gripped his biceps as she sucked in a breath and leaned into him. "I can't believe you. That's just mean—and we're in public, no less."

"Isn't that why it's so fun? Because you know anyone might notice the look of pleasure on your face, that they might catch a glimpse of my hand on your ass and realize that you're bare-assed under your dress, or they might hear your wanton whimpers as you try to hold back the screams of your orgasm." He tipped her chin up so she'd be forced to look at him...and so he could see the effect the vibe was having on her, the way her chest lifted with each shallow breath, her plump lips parted, and how her eyes slipped shut. "Sweet girl...you're so fucking gorgeous. And we both know that the fact that anyone could be watching at this very moment, that Klaus might still have his gaze fixated on you, is turning you on to no end."

"Please, Marshall...I'm going to come." If it weren't for his arm around her waist, holding her up, he had no doubt her knees would have given out on her.

When he spoke, he couldn't quite keep the humor from his voice, his lips twitching into a smile. "I can't tell if you want to come or if you don't? Which one is it, Ms. Jones? Because I could play with the controls on the remote if you wish."

"Fuck...." And then she was coming undone in his arms, quivering and trembling as the waves of her orgasm rocked her body and he held her close. Flicking off the vibe, he scooped her into his arms, loving how she held onto him, her head cradled against his neck and shoulder.

"You're so precious, Harper." He sat them down in a shadowed nook, leaving her curled up in his lap so he could hold her close, nowhere near ready to let go of her just yet. She felt perfect in his arms, and his heart hitched unexpectedly, though he was willing to blame it on the fact that he'd never wanted anyone more, his cock rock hard and aching to have her.

With her nestled in his arms and her ass resting against his hard length, Marshall shifted them so they could people-watch and take in the entertainment provided on small stages throughout the club. There were several erotic tableaus playing out, some more vanilla than others, but with every scene designed to arouse and sexually charge the atmosphere.

She shifted in his arms to look around, the movement causing her plump ass cheeks to rub invitingly against his cock. "Wow...this is some party, Marshall. They really don't hold back at these sorts of things, do they?"

"Not usually, though this is pretty mild compared to some of the other parties that'll be held this week." He brushed his cheek against hers and nipped his way down her neck, one hand gripping her hip to shift her along his hard length as his other hand slipped up her thigh, inching its way closer to her slick heat.

She covered his hand with hers and tried to push it away, even as her hips rocked against his cock. "Marshall...people will see."

"Does the thought of it turn you on?" If he had to put money on it, he bet it did. And then he spotted an all too familiar form, biting back a groan. Why did Claire insist on following him around? All the way to London, no less. "Fuck."

"What? What's wrong?" Harper glanced around the room and then turned to him, her brow creased with concern.

"Come on, sweetheart...I think it's time we moved this back to the hotel. I want you naked, with your tight body wrapped around my cock." Shifting Harper onto her feet, she pulled her dress down as far as it would go, as if trying to ignore the little fact that her underwear was in his pocket and she had a vibe stuck against her G-spot.

Standing at her side, he pulled her into his arms, covering her mouth with his, unable to resist her and wondering if he'd ever get his fill. Then, before Claire could spot them, he was moving Harper through the crowds and towards the nearest exit.

By the time they got back to their hotel room, he could barely keep his hands off her, his body thrumming with desire and on one singular track that had little to do with anything but the most primal of needs.

She gave him a flirty look over her shoulder as she pulled out of his grasp and wandered into their room, her sweet ass swaying while her gorgeous legs teetered on heels that him going even harder than he already was. "I'd say I trust you to share the bed—but I don't. Not in the least."

"Probably wise since I have every intention of making you come so hard every room on this floor will know my name." Marshall caught her hand in his and pulled her to him, slipping his arm around her waist, making it impossible to ignore the way her soft curves pressed against his body. "And before you start panicking, it doesn't have to be anything more than just one night, sweet girl."

If he had to convince her again tomorrow, then he'd do just that. Anything to make sure he had her in his arms once more.

Her eyes narrowed as she took him in, as if reading his mind. "Why do I have a feeling one night's going to turn into the whole week?"

"It will if I have anything to say about it." His hands slipped gently down her back and cupped her ass, hauling her against his hard cock as he nipped and nibbled on her neck, so she shivered in his arms and pressed herself against him in response. He desperately wanted her, and though he knew she wanted to keep her distance, it was clear she wanted him too. He just needed her to throw caution to the wind, and give in to what was between them, instead of constantly overthinking things. Because the truth was, they both needed this thing between them, and there was no denying it.

She let out a needy moan when he trailed bites and kisses down her neck, her back arching in his arms as the lingering scent of her perfume filled his head and spurred him on. He nipped on her breasts through the fabric, catching her nipples between his teeth, first one and then the other, feeling the nubs of flesh tighten and harden in his mouth.

Shifting her back, he pinned her against the wall, catching her mouth in a hard kiss as he lifted her arms above her head and held them there in the grip of one hand, as his other hand skimmed down her body, pausing to run his thumb over her nipple before giving it a pinch and a tug.

She arched against him and bit back a needy moan in response, clearly wanting him as badly as he wanted her. "How is it you always manage to convince me to stray off the path I'm determined to stay on?"

"It's because the path you're so determined to stay on is not the path you truly want to be on." He tipped her chin up and bit her lip, his eyes locked on hers and filled with humor. "You see, Ms. Jones...the path you want is the one that leads to you in my bed naked. And since we both know it to be the truth, there's little point in denying it."

"Okay...you might be right, but that doesn't mean this isn't a stupid idea."

"Sweet girl, we're both far from stupid, and there's nothing wrong with enjoying ourselves." He'd been craving her since their one time together, and it left him desperate to have her once more.

Yanking her dress up off her head, he took but a minute to appreciate the pretty black and pink lace bra that allowed him to see her pert nipples through the diaphanous fabric, before he flicked the clasp open and tossed it aside, leaving her naked to his touch.

His hands slipped up the sides of her waist until he could run his thumbs under the swell of her breasts before shifting further up to tease her nipples. He loved seeing her breath catch...loved to see her need for him override her determination to keep her distance.

"I bet you just love the fact that I can't resist you." She glared at him, but her anger held no heat and was short-lived, extinguished when he sucked her nipple into his mouth and let his fingers glide up her inner thighs to slowly stroke her clit, her sex slick and ready for him.

"Do you think it's easy for me to stay away from you? Don't you think I've tried? Well, I have, Harper—and I've failed miserably, which means that if I can't stay away, if I can't keep myself from wanting you, then my only alternative is to do everything in my power to have you." He scoffed at just how true his words were with a frustrated shake of his head. Not having her just wasn't an option. "On your knees, Ms. Jones."

"Damn it...why does that turn me on?" With nimble fingers, she unbuttoned his shirt, letting him shrug out of it, as she worked the button and zipper on his jeans, freeing his cock and stroking him. With her still standing before him, he caught her mouth in a hungry kiss as her hand slipped its way up his erect shaft, her thumb circling the head of his cock and smearing the pre-cum down the crease. "You make me crazy, Marshall."

"Ms. Jones...crazy will be the least of your worries when I have you tied to the bed and I'm paddling your ass for disobeying me earlier. Now get on your knees, sweet girl, before you make matters worse for yourself." Fuck...he didn't know what had gotten into him, but Harper had it so he couldn't think straight.

Maybe it was because all the years he'd spent with Claire were years spent compromising, her needs far more vanilla than his own. Not that he was into anything extreme. But, fucking hell...sex with Claire had been...lifeless and uninspired. And not for lack of trying—on his part at least. As for Claire and her efforts—well, she was too busy screwing around behind his back to have any real interest in his needs.

And then there was Harper, who made him feel free and left him feeling uninhibited. She reminded him what it was like to truly want sex, to truly enjoy it and relish it—but there was more between them...so much more.

Harper pushed him back towards the bed, shifting his jeans down over his hips so he could kick them off and toss them aside, leaving him naked and erect before her. Slowly, with her hands running down his body and his cock slipping between her full breasts, she got to her knees and nuzzled his cock with her cheek as she looked up at him, her lips brushing against his delicate skin. "Is this what you want?"

"It's a good start." And when she ran her tongue up the length of his shaft and then wrapped her lips around his cock, it was even better. "That's it, Ms. Jones..."

Unable to pull his gaze away, he watched her suck him, her lips stretched around his girth, as she took a little more of him with each pass while her hands worked down his shaft. Fuck, she was gorgeous, and the fact that she couldn't resist him, that she wanted him so honestly, for the sheer pleasure of it, only added to the moment.

Tangling his fingers in her hair, he fisted her mahogany locks, loving the control it gave him, loving that he could set the pace and could decide just how much of him she'd take. And when she let out a needy moan in response, the vibrations it sent humming against his cock had him thrusting his hips forward as she eagerly took him.

"Harper...that's so fucking good." He couldn't help but

fuck her mouth, his cock slipping in and out past her lips as his pace quickened, her fingers stroking his balls and that tender spot just behind them. He could feel the pressure building at this core, every nerve in his body thrumming with energy as he rode that razor's edge, his orgasm racing right at him. "I'm going to come, love. You have me so close."

And then she did something with her tongue and he was done for. With a primal grunt, his body tensed as he thrust into her mouth, his cock pulsing his hot cum down her throat as she eagerly swallowed it, his breathing ragged and heavy as the vision of her on her knees seared itself in his head. "That...was...fucking hell, Harper...that was amazing."

"Quid pro quo, Clarice." Her Silence of the Lambs reference had him biting back a laugh as she got to her feet and pushed him back onto the bed so she could straddle him. The fact that she was so eager to play, that she wanted more, and was willing to take what she wanted was such a fucking turn-on.

With her kneeling on the bed by his side, he stroked her clit and then, slipping his fingers deep inside her, he hooked the loop on the plug and slowly pulled it out of her tight pussy as he swallowed her needy moans with a hungry kiss. Tossing the plug aside, he laid back and grabbed her hand, pulling her to him and positioning her so she now straddled his face, giving him access to her sweet cunt.

"Is this what you want, love?" Gripping her hips, he pulled her to him, running his tongue along her slick slit, her juices salty sweet on his tongue as he parted her soft folds and flicked at her clit. She was so fucking wet for him, and it turned him on to no end to know that she'd enjoyed blowing him.

"Most definitely." Her breath caught and she bit her lip as her hips rocked against him, her fingers tangling in his hair as if she was holding on to him, her body tensing with each flick of his tongue.

Reaching up, he teased her nipple and sucked on her clit, causing her pace to quicken as she reached back and stroked his cock and he went hard for her once more. Fucking her with his tongue, her thighs tightened as he pushed her towards her orgasm, gripping her ass and pulling her closer, deeper, her moans spurring him on. And then she was quivering against him as she cried out his name, her orgasm tearing through her as he milked the last of it from her sweet body until her breathing finally slowed back to normal.

Her lips kicked up in a mischievous smile as she looked down at him. "Not only are you fantastic with your cock, but you're also pretty damn amazing with that mouth of yours. And that bit of stubble...don't ever shave it off."

He couldn't help but laugh as he shifted her off him and onto her hands and knees, giving her a playful slap across the ass, his cock already aching to have her. Grabbing his jeans up off the floor, he dug out a condom and sheathed himself, pushing thoughts of taking her bare from his mind, even if he'd like nothing more than to sink into her, skin to skin. Tight as she was, he knew it'd feel fucking amazing. Yet the last thing he needed was to have two women pregnant with his children, and at the same time no less. Unfortunately, after Claire, he wasn't quite ready to give anyone that sort of trust. Not yet, anyway.

Kneeling by Harper's side, he fisted her hair and gently pulled her head back so he could kiss her, his tongue darting past her lips as he swallowed her needy moans. "Tell me you want this, Harper."

"I do, Marshall...I want you more than is wise." She bit her bottom lip and arched her back as he let go of her hair and let his fingers dance down her spine to her perfectly plump ass.

Shifting so that his thighs brushed against hers, he grabbed his erect cock and slipped the head of it against her slit, working it from her clit to her ass and back again, teasing her until he could take no more. With a tilt of his hips, he sunk his cock into her, taking her with one go, forcing her tight little body to stretch around his thick cock. "You feel so fucking good, Harper... If I were to die tomorrow, I swear, I'd die a happy man after having your sweet cunt."

She looked over her shoulder at him, her brow furrowed. "Don't say things like that, Marshall."

He didn't quite understand what he'd said to upset her, but he suddenly felt like an ass, even if he didn't know why. "Harper...hey, are you okay?"

"No. But I want you to fuck me anyway." She shook her head as if to clear it, but he couldn't bear to continue. Pulling out of her, he pulled her into his arms, even as she fought him. "I need you not to stop. Please...for me."

Fucking hell...he didn't know what the hell to do. Whatever he'd said had upset her, yet it was also clear she needed the physical connection. Thoughts of taking her rough and hard disappeared as he gently turned her onto her back, and nestled himself between her legs, burying himself deep inside her once more, though this time they were face to face. "It's okay, love...I've got you."

Harper sank into Marshall's arms as he held her tightly

to him, her body stretched tight around his cock as he filled her, taking her slow and sweet, hoping to comfort her when she looked so broken. In that moment, he wanted nothing more than to protect her and keep her safe, to keep the darkness away, and try to make her happy. And so he kissed her like nothing in the world mattered but the two of them.

She clung to him; his forehead lowered to hers as their pace quickened and he covered her face in his kisses, her legs wrapped around his thighs, pulling him deeper. He tilted his hips so each thrust was intense and with purpose, the energy inside him starting to build once more, as his head spun with heightened emotions, his connection to Harper unlike anything he'd felt before.

Hooking her leg behind the knee, he opened her up to him, so he could bury himself fully with each thrust, filling her completely while pressing against that sweet spot deep inside her, her little moans of pleasure pushing him so he was teetering on the edge of coming again. And then he bit her neck, the flicker of pain enough to set her orgasm free, making her cry out as she clung to him and her body quivered in his arms.

A few more hard thrusts unleashed his own release like lightning in a summer storm, his cock pulsing deep inside her as he came. With their breathing still heavy and his pulse hammering, they lay there, their bodies entwined until he slowly pulled out of her, discarding the condom before he gathered her into his arms.

He was still feeling fiercely protective of her, hating that there were things in her life that could bring her to tears. And it didn't matter that he'd only known her less than a year and they'd only gotten together recently, or that they weren't supposed to be taking things seriously.

In that moment, she was all he cared about.

CHAPTER 12

Harper couldn't believe she'd let such a small thing get to her. She felt like a fool for overreacting, even if Marshall had been incredibly sweet about it all. He'd somehow managed to soothe her jagged nerves and ease the pain in her heart, and she swore, he claimed a little piece of her soul in that moment.

Holding her to him, Marshall swept the hair from her shoulder and kissed the top of her head. "Harper...I'm here for you if you want to talk."

She wanted to pull out of his arms and escape so that she wouldn't have to discuss this, but his hold on her tightened as if he'd read her mind. "There's nothing to discuss. I'm fine. And that's not what this relationship is."

She knew that if she told him, it would change the dynamic of what was between them. If he knew, he'd look at her as if she was broken and fragile, and then he'd handle her with kid gloves. She was having fun for once and the last thing she wanted was for him to start pitying her.

"Maybe not, but I meant it when I said that I wanted to get to know you better—and if there's something bothering you, then maybe I can help." He let out a breath ragged with frustration.

"You can't help. No one can. And getting to know me was not part of our deal. My life is my own, and I'm not saying that to be a bitch. My life is just too screwed up for me to rehash all my issues and not have you look at me differently." She shifted closer and stole a lingering kiss, feeling some of his frustration with her ease. "I honestly need a bit of a break from my life, and I was hoping this week away in London would give me a few days where I could escape everything that haunts me. Discussing my problems will defeat all of that, which is why I can't."

"I get it, Harper...I honestly do. But...just know that if you do feel like you need to talk, I'm here for you." He ran his hand over her hair and kissed the top of her head. "Believe it or not, I'm a pretty good listener."

As a doctor, she imagined he'd had an excellent bedside manner, immediately setting his patients and their families at ease. "Your patients must have loved you."

"They did." His smile kicked up as he gave her a shrug, still holding her close to him. "And the truth is, I really do miss it, though I love what I'm doing at Clio too."

"How on earth did you get started with Clio? It just seems so different than being a surgeon." She couldn't imagine making such a drastic change to her life.

"When I was in college, I had this girlfriend who was a little bit...adventurous. But one of the things she always complained about was how crappy the sex toys on the market were. I guess that always stuck with me. I like figuring things out and tinkering with things—was actually an engineering student when I first started college.

Afterwards, my medical knowledge sort of gave me a different perspective, so when I came up with an idea, I hired an engineer to bring the design to life." He gave her a smile that lit up his eyes, though after a moment, his smile faded. "I was sort of pursuing both Clio and my practice, but after Claire and what happened, I couldn't stay at the hospital and my practice. I'd end up fucking murdering the asshole my wife was screwing if I had to see him every day."

"So you decided to focus on just Clio." It was more of a conclusion than a question. Clio was still a fairly young company, though it certainly seemed like Marshall's divorce was getting dragged out.

"It'd be even better if Claire would stop showing up at my office and would just sign the divorce papers, but she wants to make me miserable, and has a knack for doing just that." He stole a quick kiss and then snuggled her in his arms. "Sleep, sweet girl. We've got a long day ahead of us."

"I suppose I won't make you sleep on the sofa after all— as long as you behave yourself."

His smile kicked up and he stole another kiss, rolling her under him as he nestled himself between her legs once more. "Never, Ms. Jones."

***

"So, what's the plan? Do you need me to keep an eye out for anything in particular?" Sitting on the edge of the bed, in nothing but her lingerie, Harper slipped on her silk stockings and stood so she could clip them to her garter, thinking it was a good thing she'd thought to pack something sexy.

"Damn, Harper...maybe we can just stay here instead. You look fucking amazing." Marshall bit his bottom lip, looking ready to devour her as he closed the distance between them, his body sidling up to hers as his hands grasped her hips and pulled her to him. His cheek was rough against hers as he nipped at her ear, his warm breath sending a shiver of need down her spine, making her want him yet again, even if she was already tender from him taking her through the night.

"Work, Marshall. That's why we're here." Somehow she found the strength to push him away, her hand firm on his muscular chest. "And I'm not guaranteeing that last night's going to become a regular occurrence."

He shook his head with a laugh. "Sweet girl...keep telling yourself that if it makes you feel any better. But this week? You're all mine."

When his hands tightened on her hips and he caught her mouth in a hard kiss, she fisted the fabric of his shirt, holding onto him as his tongue danced with hers, sending a wave of need straight through her, making her go wet with need. She couldn't remember ever wanting anyone the way she wanted Marshall—and it was pointless to pretend otherwise.

Never in a million years had she imagined finding herself in this sort of situation. She couldn't help but think of Josh and the sort of relationship they had, which had been fantastic, but...nothing this exciting or edgy. And she felt guilty for actually enjoying herself—which she was, even if she had her doubts about what she was doing and how wise it was.

Her breathing was heavy by the time she finally managed to pull away. "Fine...one week. But after that I need my old job back, because there's no way I'll be able to work with you and not want you."

"We'll start with a week, and once we're back, we'll find a way to work together." Marshall stole another kiss before his lips trailed down her neck, nipping and biting at her shoulder, her needy moans escaping her lips as her body thrummed with desire. "You just love that flicker of pain, don't you?"

"You know I do." And if they kept this up, they'd never get to the conference—her point proved when he sat down on the edge of the bed and pulled her into his lap, draping her over his muscular thighs with her ass in the air as her heart beat out a staccato.

"And what about this?" He slapped her ass hard enough to have the skin stinging, though only for a second, before it turned into a heat that had her going wet and desperately wanting more. "Do you like that, too?"

She bit her lip as she felt herself go wet, nodding in answer since she knew it'd be easy enough for him to check. "Yeah...I do."

The next blow fell on the other cheek, harder this time, so she couldn't keep her needy cry silent, her clit aching for attention as he ran his hand over her warmed skin. "More, Ms. Jones?"

She wanted to groan, despite knowing that she had to give him an answer, especially if she wanted him to continue. "Please."

"Such a polite little thing." This time one slap fell right after the other, harder than before, so it took the sting longer to mellow into the pleasure she was craving, though her clit was now throbbing as she squeezed her thighs together, looking for some relief. His hand soothed her ass cheeks before slipping down over her sex, shifting her soaked panties to the side, even though he made no effort to slip his fingers inside her, which only added to how badly she wanted him to do just that. "You're so wet, love."

There was no denying it. And when the next few blows landed, each harder than the one before, she swore she'd come simply from him spanking her. She wasn't only wet, but crazy with desperation, needing him to take her hard and make her come. "Marshall...please...I need you to fuck me."

Instead, he helped her to her feet, leaving her with her hair disheveled, her cheeks on both her face and ass flaming hot, and her pussy aching so badly with need that it hurt. "Why would I do that when I can have you aching for me all day long? I want you to feel my hand on your ass with each step you take, and each time you sit down. And when I do finally take you, sweet girl, I want you to be crazed with wanting me."

She knew, without a doubt, that he was right about the effect he'd have on her throughout the day. The mere thought of it was enough to have her begging for him to give her some relief. "That's just mean, Marshall. Please...just one little orgasm?"

"Now where would the fun in that be?" He stood up, looking so sexy that it made her heart hitch. Tilting her chin up, he stole a chaste kiss and then knelt before her, his large capable hands slipping down her calves as he helped her slide into her heels, before stepping away from her with a satisfied smile, her body reeling from his absence. "Get dressed, Ms. Jones. I do believe we have a conference to attend."

CHAPTER 13

With Harper at his side, Marshall slipped his hand down to the small of her back, letting it settle there as they walked around the conference. Even though they were there to work, he found himself needing some sort of physical connection to her, since he was still hard for her from earlier.

He just couldn't get the vision of her draped over his lap out of his head, the porcelain skin of her plump ass marked red with his handprints. It left him desperate to find an empty room where he could take her hard against the wall, or maybe skip the conference altogether and drag her back up to their room.

"Wow. I had no idea it'd be so busy." She looked up at him with a smile before taking another look around. He didn't think Harper had been to many conferences at all, let alone one related to the adult novelty industry. "There are some...interesting things here."

"That's a bit of an understatement, Ms. Jones." There was everything from sex toys to adult entertainment, lingerie to kink and fetish—and everything in between. Many were dressed in casual business attire, but there were far more who were scantily clad at best, especially when dealing with the adult film industry. Though Harper was far less innocent than he'd first thought her to be, he had to wonder how comfortable she was with some of the stuff on display. "We'll just wander for now. See if anything looks interesting. And if any ideas come to you, make sure you tell me right away so we can jot it down and revisit it later, since it's too easy for ideas to come and go so quickly that they can be impossible to recall once it slips your mind."

She grabbed his arm with a huge smile, her grey eyes alight with excitement so they flickered with sparks of blue. "I know exactly what you mean. It seems like I always get ideas while I'm in the shower or just as I'm falling asleep. I have to keep a pad of paper by my bedside. And did you know they make pads of waterproof paper? It's an absolutely brilliant idea, if you ask me."

Loving her enthusiasm, he pulled her close and kissed her forehead, not caring if anyone saw them—and someone most certainly did. "Fuck. Claire...what the hell are you doing here?"

His ex swaggered over to them on precariously high heels with daggers in her eyes aimed at Harper, as Marshall stood there with his arm still around her waist. And though Claire looked like she always had with bleached blonde locks, perfectly applied makeup, and a skin-hugging designer dress that showed off far too much of what she had to offer, she suddenly looked fake and overdone, compared to Harper's natural and easy beauty. "Why wouldn't I be here, Marshall? After all, you are my husband—and I want to stay on top of things for when Clio's mine."

Marshall's temper had him seeing red. He took a step

forward so he towered over her, even as Harper tugged on his arm, begging him to leave it. "That's never going to happen. I'll fucking burn Clio to the ground before I ever give any of it over to you."

"Is that a threat, Marshall?" Claire was forced to take a step back, her eyes going wide for a moment as if she hadn't expected to piss him off. In truth, he'd never had much of a temper, but she was finding new ways to make him angry.

"Take it any way you want, Claire. But Clio will never end up in your cheating, money-grubbing hands." He'd had enough, his anger like poison in his veins, every muscle tense. He grabbed Harper's hand and turned to go, but Claire clearly wasn't done.

"I can't believe it. You're actually with her?" Claire threw her head back and laughed. "Marshall, I've got to tell you...you really have hit rock bottom. Not that I'm surprised. After all—I was always the best thing about you. And let's face it, it's not like this plain-Jane will be able to satisfy you—not with your edgy tastes."

Marshall spun around, moving into her space so she was forced to step back, his hands curled into fists as he forced his words past his clenched jaw. "You could only hope to be as amazing as Harper, both in and out of the bedroom—but you'll never be. Because I know you, Claire, and you're nothing but a nasty and ugly conniving bitch who only cares about herself. The day I'm rid of you will be the happiest fucking day of my life."

He left her there stammering for a comeback and stomping her foot, as he walked towards the nearest exit with Harper on his arm, needing to put some distance between himself and Claire before he did something he regretted. When they got to the lobby, he slowed to a stop and pulled Harper into his arms, cupping her face, worried about her. "Are you okay?"

"Me? Are you kidding? You're the one who just had to go another round with Medusa." She shook her head as if trying to clear it from all that'd just happened. "She can say all she wants about me, Marshall. I'm fine with who I am, and know better than to let nasty people drag me down."

He loved that she wasn't fazed by Claire's nastiness—but he was still worried that dealing with his ex would end up being too much crazy for Harper to handle, when it'd just be easier to walk away from him and whatever it was they were doing. And if she did, it wasn't like he could blame her. He wouldn't wish Claire on his worst enemy.

"I need some fresh air. Do you mind if we go for a walk?" If not, he supposed dragging her up to their room to burn through some of his frustration might be a good alternative.

She nodded, and then went up onto the tips of her toes to gently kiss his cheek, her soft curves brushing against his body. "I think that'd be lovely."

It turned out to be a gorgeous spring day. London was bustling with people, but there was a park nearby with gorgeous gardens and plenty of paths and park benches. Flowers of every color lined the walkways as trees stretched their branches overhead. But it was the smell of damp earth that calmed him, reminding him of the woods around his home where he liked to hike.

He twined his fingers with hers as they lazily walked hand in hand down the different paths, his anger a mere shadow of what it'd been with Harper's calming presence. Steering them towards a park bench, he pulled her into his lap and wrapped his arms around her waist while he took her in, her thick mahogany hair catching the light so it shimmered red in the sunlight, and her grey eyes shifted to blue.

"You're stunning, you know." He couldn't hold back the words.

Her lips quirked into a smile as she slipped her arms around his neck, her skin soft and warm. "I like that you say it as if it's a fact."

"That's because it is, sweet girl. No one in their right mind would think otherwise. It's why Claire's so jealous of you." Marshall needed her to know just how special she was—because she truly was, combining beauty and brains, with a personality that mixed confidence and humor with kindness. "You're gorgeous, smart, and vibrant—genuine too. And she's nothing but an ugly, manipulative, and greedy bitch."

"I have to say, Marshall...you're one of the sweetest guys I've met. But this thing with your ex is beyond crazy." She cupped his cheek and then leaned in to kiss him, her lips lingering on his as she shifted in his lap, making him hard.

"I'm sorry you've had to deal with her. But I promise, I'll make it up to you as soon as we get back to the hotel." Grabbing her hips, he pulled her to him so her plump ass rode against his cock, as he bit her lip and thought about taking her once more, not just because he desperately wanted Harper, but because he wanted to eliminate any uncertainties that may exist between them after Claire's nastiness. He couldn't believe Claire had brought up his sexual preferences—as if she'd ever been adventurous.

"I'm going to hold you to that, Marshall. But work first." She slipped off his lap with a flirty smile. "We haven't really had a chance to check out the conference, and I need all the inspiration I can get if I have any hope at all of helping you figure out something new and innovative."

He took her hand as they started heading back towards the hotel, and brought it to his lips. "I have no doubt you're capable of it, whether we go to the conference or not."

"Although...I suppose with Claire running around loose, maybe waiting isn't a bad idea. No offense but...I can't believe you married her." Harper gave him a sideways glance and a shake of her head, as if she thought him insane. "Was she always like that?"

"No. Nothing like that, though it's now clear it was all a lie from the very start." He couldn't believe he'd fallen for her act. That was the worst part of the whole thing.

"Marshall...do you think she'd do anything crazy? It just seems odd that she's shown up here—and she had also been at your office again before we'd left." Harper looked a little uneasy, as if he might get upset with her for questioning Claire's sanity.

"She's more vindictive than crazy—like she's pissed off at me for catching her cheating and it's my fault I ruined the nice gig she had going. Doctor's wife, parties to attend, and plenty of money so she could quit her job—which is exactly what she did just a few months after we got married. Which I was fine with. She wanted to start a fashion blog, and I had my practice to deal with, so I figured it'd help keep her busy." Except that she decided she'd rather spend her time fucking someone else while he was working, and then telling him a bunch of lies when he got home. "But what really pushed her over the edge was when the court ruled in my favor where Clio was concerned. I was ordered to pay her a small monetary amount, but Clio's mine, even if she refuses to believe it."

Their walking slowed to a stop as Harper turned to look at him, her brow creased with worry and her eyes clouding to a stormy grey. "She sounds delusional, Marshall. Are you sure she's not crazy enough to do something extreme?"

He let out a deep breath and ran a rough hand through his hair, trying to figure out just how far Claire would escalate things. "I think for now, she's just happy to keep shadowing my every move so she can make me crazy."

"And the mole...you don't think it's her?" Harper crinkled her nose as if unsure about bringing up the subject and accusing his ex.

"I've certainly thought about it, but other than showing up to my office, the rest of Clio is under lock and key, and my idea files are password protected on my laptop and on the server at Clio. She wouldn't have access to the sort of information that's made it into our competitors' hands, which means there's someone on the inside who's betrayed us."

"But who would do such a thing, Marshall? I can't even imagine someone at Clio stooping so low." She looked genuinely worried, and it claimed a piece of his heart.

Cupping the back of her neck, he pulled her to him and pressed a kiss to her forehead. "Don't worry about it, sweet girl. I'm looking into it as we speak."

CHAPTER 14

The run-in with Claire at the hotel had left Harper feeling a bit unsure about her relationship with Marshall, even if he'd done a good job of settling most of her worries. She told herself that it didn't really matter anyway—that this thing with Marshall was nothing but a bit of fun. Except that she knew that was nothing but a lie. She was already falling for Marshall, faster and harder than was wise.

"You're awfully quiet, sunshine." Marshall pulled her close and pressed a kiss to her temple as they continued heading towards the hotel, the sidewalks bustling with people. "I'm worried about you."

It was sweet of Marshall to be so concerned about her, especially when she'd felt so alone and on her own these last few years. She couldn't really deny that she was falling for Marshall despite her best efforts to keep him at bay, and if she were being honest with herself, she wanted to push aside her worries and just live in the moment.

She wanted to enjoy herself for once—and she wanted Marshall without having to constantly second-guess herself and what they were doing. And why shouldn't she want him? He was unlike any guy she'd ever known: sweet, smart, considerate, sexy... She might be telling herself that their timing was off and that he was her boss, but...she was tired of fighting the darkness and he might be just what she needed to finally find the light again.

With a newfound determination, she gave Marshall a smile and slipped her arm around his waist, nestling against his side as he put his arm around her shoulder. "I know you've been worried about me, but you know...I think I'm okay—for the first time in a long while."

He glanced down at her with a questioning glance, as if not quite believing it, before leaning in to steal a kiss as he maneuvered them around the crowds. "I can't tell you how happy a man that makes me, Harper. It's nice to see you looking so...at peace."

"We deserve to be happy, right?" Why the hell not? And now that she'd made up her mind, she was determined not to let things—like Claire's manipulations—muck things up. She still wasn't sure what she had with Marshall, whether it was still something casual or if it was turning into something more serious, and for once she was okay with that. She was happy to just live in the moment and enjoy what was between them—whatever that happened to be.

"We definitely deserve it—and it's been a long time coming for the both of us."

***

By the time they got back to the convention, it was truly in full swing, with the amount of attendees having tripled. In a way, Harper was glad for the crowds, since it allowed them to become just one of many, so that if Claire was still around, it'd be more difficult for her to find and keep track of them.

They wandered from table to table, taking in the huge selection of products on display, though much of it had nothing to do with the type of products Clio developed. And one thing was clear—as sexy as Marshall was, he could have had a damn good time if he'd come here on his own, something he no doubt was fully aware of, having attended this conference before.

She'd lost count of the number of women who'd given Marshall a head-to-toe look—and had been none too subtle about it either, even though he'd linked his fingers with hers and would regularly pull her close to say something to her or point out a product, his head bent to hers in a gesture of intimate familiarity. And each time he did, their bodies would brush against each other, reminding her of what it was like to be on the receiving end of his attention.

"Harper!"

She looked around, wondering who the hell would know her here, when she spotted her friend, Ben, moving in her direction. With a huge smile, Ben pulled her into a big hug and gave her a kiss on the cheek.

"I didn't realize you'd be here." Harper shifted out of Ben's arms and introduced him to Marshall. "Ben's actually the reason I applied to Clio. He'd heard Clio was hiring and sent me your way."

Marshall shook his hand. "I'll have to thank you for sending us Harper. She's been an invaluable asset. And you're also an engineer? For Titan?"

"I am. They wanted me along to answer any of the more technical questions people might have." Ben looked at Marshall, bright-eyed. "So you're the guy who started Clio.

Wow...I've got to say, I've been a fan. Your company's been making some great products."

"Well, Titan's been some of our toughest competition." Marshall's focus remained intently on Ben, even if he seemed pretty relaxed otherwise.

"We'll need to catch up, Harper. Maybe grab dinner and a few drinks?" Ben gave her a far too hopeful look, clearly not realizing that Marshall was a little more than just her boss. "I hate the crowds at these sort of events, but I'm only at the table for the early shift, so I've got the afternoons and evenings off."

She looked over at Marshall in apology. "I don't think I'll be able to get away, Ben."

Marshall shook his head. "You should go out to dinner with your friend—maybe tomorrow?"

"Yeah...I guess. If we're not busy." Harper was feeling a bit confused, since Ben had clearly made no secret of his interest in her. "I've got your cell number. I'll text you and let you know."

"Perfect." With a huge smile, he kissed her cheek, and then shook Marshall's hand. "It was a pleasure."

After their discussion in the park, she wasn't quite sure why he'd try to push her into dinner with Ben, although maybe Marshall was just trying to make sure she knew that he was fine with it. Which was great that he wasn't a controlling ass—except that she found that she really didn't want to go if it meant being away from him.

Or was he trying to get rid of her for the evening so he could have some time to himself? Without her, he could easily have all sorts of fun and take full advantage of the trouble he could get himself into with so many willing participants vying for his attention. She didn't think it was really the case, but so many of the women were gorgeous and clearly interested, while she'd done nothing but fight him tooth and nail—even if she'd finally come around. Maybe Claire's dig about Harper not being able to satisfy Marshall had actually dug deeper than she thought, and she was now being paranoid.

Grabbing her hand, he led her through the crowds, though they were going too fast to really look at anything— and it was then that she realized something was up, worry snaking its way into her chest. Far too noisy to carry on any sort of real conversation, Marshall pulled her towards the lobby and into a quiet corner.

When he finally slowed to a stop and turned to her, his tone held an edge she didn't quite understand. "How well do you know Ben?"

Her eyes narrowed at him as she tried to figure out what exactly was going on. "What do you mean? 'Cause if you're wondering if we'd dated, the answer is yes—though it was only a handful of dates and that was about seven years ago."

"That's not what I meant, since it was already clear from the way he looked at you that you'd been intimate with each other at one point or another." He shook his head, though his eyes had clouded over and he was feeling closed off, so she couldn't really get a read on what he was thinking.

"So then...what? I don't understand what you're asking me."

"Titan is one of the companies that I'm convinced has some of our designs. And...I don't know. I guess I'm being paranoid." He shook his head as if to clear it, letting out a deep breath as he pulled her to him and stole a sweet, lingering kiss, though she could feel the tension in his every move.

She still didn't quite understand what he was asking her, nor did she fully understand what he was implying. But his kiss soothed her worries, leaving her standing in his arms as she tried to sort through Marshall's suspicions. "Ben would never do something like steal our secrets—and he lives in California. I haven't even seen him since we graduated, if you're thinking that he somehow used me to get into Clio."

He brushed his thumb across her cheek, his fingers tangling in her hair as he bent his head to hers, his touch warm and the closeness of his body comforting. "I'm sorry, Harper. I swear, I thought I could set aside my problems, but the whole thing with there being a mole at Clio is still making me crazy, even if I know we should be trying to enjoy the time we have here in London."

But there was still something she just didn't understand. "I know you have a lot on your mind, Marshall—and I get that you can't just let it go. Finding the mole is really important. But then why suggest I go out to dinner with Ben if you suspected he might have something to do with the stolen designs?"

His brow furrowed as he took her in, cupping her cheek as his gold eyes locked on hers, the intensity of his gaze stealing her breath. "Because I wasn't thinking straight. I hated the thought that you and Ben had been together— especially when it's clear that he still wants you. But being jealous of you with another man also caught me off guard when I promised you I'd keep this fun and casual—although the truth is that I really do want something more serious with you."

"Do you really? Or is it just jealousy because I've been intimate with Ben?" Her heart tugged at the thought, and she knew in that moment that her head might be saying she didn't want anything but a bit of fun, but her heart was wanting a whole lot more from him. Suddenly it all felt like a giant leap to take—and it had her heart racing with a panic she was doing her best to beat into submission.

"It'd be easy to blame it on simple jealousy and not wanting anyone else to be with you. But you know that I really like you, Harper. I have from the moment you started working at Clio. Like you said, we deserve to be happy, and there's no way I'm letting things come to an end between us once this week is over." He tightened his hold on her, nuzzling her with his forehead bent to hers. "I can't give you up, Harper. I want you to be mine. So if you think this is something casual that you can just walk away from, you can guess again. Because this thing between us? There's nothing casual about it. There never was."

And then he was kissing her, his mouth plundering hers as his hands tangled in her hair, her body coming alive as if his very touch was a live wire. Kisses turned to nips that trailed down her throat as he lifted her into his arms, her legs wrapping around his waist, ignoring the fact that they were surrounded by people. Not that she cared at that very moment, her needy whimpers refusing to be contained as he carried her through a nearby door and into the empty stairwell of the hotel.

With her legs still wrapped around his hips, he pinned her to the wall for leverage, her heart racing. Grabbing at the lace of her panties, he tore them from her body with a sharp tug, the stinging pain making her pussy gush and her head spin, as he freed his stiff cock.

She had just a moment to think of protection when he impaled her fully on his hard length, all logical thoughts vanishing in that single thrust as he claimed her like no man ever had. And then he was fucking her, fast and hard, as she clung to him, his mouth on hers, swallowing her needy cries, one thrust after another, their pace frantic and primal, spurred on by the fact that anyone could walk in on them at any moment.

Yet she could think of nothing but him, could think of nothing but coming as he sent every nerve thrumming with a building energy, his tongue darting over hers, her body trapped between his hard body and the cold wall. It was too much, too intense, and then she was crying out, coming undone in his arms as he thrust into her again and came with a grunt, his cock pulsing his cum deep inside her, their mouths and bodies locked as one.

"Fuck, Harper...I'm sorry." With his breathing ragged, he slowly pulled out of her and lowered her legs to the floor, his cum dripping out onto her thighs, as her pulse raced.

She tried not to panic... She'd been on a low dose of the Pill for medical reasons, although she didn't always consistently take it, even if she'd been good about it since she first started sleeping with Marshall. And then there was the little matter of unprotected sex, and the fact that his ex had been cheating on him. Yet he was a doctor...he'd have gotten himself checked, right?

She shifted her skirt down over her thighs, trying to slow her erratic pulse as he zippered his pants. "It was as much my fault as it was yours, Marshall. Just tell me..."

"I'm clean, Harper." He cupped her cheek in his large

hand, brushing his thumb over her skin, his brow creased with worry and his brown eyes dark. "I swear...I never..."

"I'm clean too—and I'm on the Pill." She groaned, but said it anyway. "Sort of."

"Sort of?"

CHAPTER 15

Back at their room, Marshall laid back against the pillows with Harper curled up at his side, their uninhibited passion now replaced with worry. What the hell had he been thinking? Clearly nothing but fucking her.

"It'll be okay, Harper." She'd explained to him that she'd been a bit inconsistent in the past with her pills, taking them late on the couple of times she'd forgotten them—but she'd been good about taking them since their first night together. "Given what you've said, you should be protected against pregnancy, though I'm sorry you even have to worry about it. Honestly, love...it should be completely safe, especially if you've taken them consistently in the past week and a half."

It was a huge relief, especially when Claire was insisting that she was pregnant with his child. Yet he knew that if it ever came to it, having a child with Harper would be nothing like having a child with Claire—and that might explain why the tiniest pang of disappointment flared in his chest, even though he knew it was an insane thought.

It was probably due to the fact that when he'd pictured

himself settling down, it'd be with someone nice and smart, funny, sweet and headstrong—and Harper was all those things. That said, it's not that he was in any way ready to start a family just yet—and he had no doubt Harper would strangle him for sticking her in his little fantasy for even a split second.

"Listen, love...about this scare...I need you to know that if anything ever did happen, I'd be here for you, no matter what you needed. And I know you've been dealing with some stuff, so I'll say it one more time because I need you to believe me—I'm here if you need to talk, and if you ever need help of any kind, I'll happily do what I can." The last thing he wanted was to add this pregnancy scare to everything else she already had piled on her plate.

"I'm sorry that I've been a bit all over the place, emotionally. It's just that..." She let out a ragged sigh. "My past, my family...I'm sure you know what it's like."

When she squeezed her eyes shut, he pulled her into his arms so she could settle against his chest, her emotions already riding so close to the surface with the mere mention of her problems. "My life's been far from perfect, Harper, so I get it. I know how hard it is to open up about that sort of thing. But it does help—and I can't bear to see you like this."

"I wasn't always like this, you know. I used to be happy. Not a care in the world." Her voice cracked, but she shook it off with a ragged breath. "I was engaged...to a wonderful man."

Marshall's heart broke for her. He knew, upset as she was, that it couldn't have ended well. "Harper...I'm so sorry. What happened?" No matter what it was, one thing was clear—the guy was a goddamned fool.

"Josh was an aeronautical engineer, and had gone up in a new plane he'd designed. He was an experienced pilot— had gone up a million times before. But...I don't know what happened. Maybe it was the new design or the engine... Anyway, something went wrong, and his plane went down."

The plane...no wonder she'd been so scared of flying.

"Sweetness...I'm so fucking sorry. I don't even know what to say." He couldn't even imagine how devastated she must have been.

"He actually managed to survive the crash itself, but...he was badly injured. It changed everything, Marshall—it changed him. The accident confined him to a wheelchair, and the pain has been unbearable. I wanted to help him...wanted to help him through it all, but he broke off our engagement...moved out, wouldn't see me or return my calls. Still won't." She angrily swiped at her tears as they escaped, though whether her anger was with her ex or because her emotions had gotten the better of her, he didn't know. Not that it mattered. All he could think of was holding her close and protecting her, even if her hurt had started long before he came into the picture. "The pain, the nightmares, the accident...they changed him into a different man. I know it's been three years, but he's still living that nightmare. He's all alone—and he won't let me help him."

"I don't even know what to say, Harper." He couldn't imagine what she must have gone through. One moment she was engaged and happy, looking forward to getting married and starting a new life, a family, and the next, her dreams and future were shattered to pieces. As a doctor, he knew the sort of effect a severe accident and chronic pain could have on a person, and unfortunately, it didn't surprise him that her fiancé had pushed her away, no doubt hurt and angry with the world.

"He became a completely different person, Marshall. And yet I still feel guilty that we didn't find a way to get through it together." She let out a shuddering breath as he cupped her face in his hands and dried her cheeks, making him wish he could somehow shield her from the pain and heartache.

"It's not as though you didn't try repeatedly to reach out to him and help him through it, Harper. You can't blame yourself when you did all you could." He tucked her in tightly against him, and kissed the top of her head. "You need to try to let it go, love. You're too young to let something like that keep you from moving on with your life."

"I wish that was everything, Marshall, but it's not. I swear, it sometimes feels like it's one thing after another." She twined her fingers with his, and even though it was a small and simple gesture, it meant a lot that she was reaching out and opening up to him. "My dad...he's been a mess ever since my mom died—and that was back when I was in high school. But she was his everything, and he's been...I don't know...I guess he's been lost without her. He drinks too much, barely leaves the house...I do what I can to help, but it's never been enough to help him get past her death, though I suppose it doesn't help that I look just like her."

"Fuck, Harper...I truly am sorry you've had to deal with so much. I know there's nothing I can say to make you feel better, but if there's anything I can do—anything at all—I'm here for you. No one should have to go through this alone." If her mother was anything like Harper, then he could see why her dad would have such a hard time getting over her.

And just like that, he realized that he was well on his way to falling for the woman in his arms.

"How do you help someone who doesn't want help? Someone who doesn't see that they're killing themselves—and dragging everyone down with them?" The weariness in her voice pissed him off. Had she been dealing with this all alone? And what exactly had she been dealing with?

Marshall couldn't help but think of his own drunk and abusive father, and the thought of her living through the nightmare he and his siblings had gone through left him furious. "I get that your dad misses your mom, but...I know what it's like to have a father who drinks too much. Just tell me he didn't fucking abuse you as a result of his drinking—'cause that's not something anyone should have to go through, whether it's physically or mentally."

She sat up out of his arms, worry creasing her brow as she shook her head. "No, he was never like that. Just melancholic and withdrawn. I've been desperate to get him into rehab before he drinks himself to death—or worse, he finds a faster method than the bottle—but I haven't managed it, so I just try my best. But..." She reached up and cupped his cheek. "I'm so sorry you had to go through all that with your father, Marshall. It's just not right."

Marshall never really talked about it much, and the truth was that he'd probably escaped the worst of it, compared to what his brothers and sisters had endured. Yet with Harper, he felt compelled to open up to her since she'd already shared so much of herself with him. "I was already off to college by the time he got really bad, and luckily he's no longer in our lives. After my brother, Jake, nearly put him in the hospital for going after my sister, we did our best to sever our ties with him."

"I can't even imagine having to put up with something like that. I'm just glad you were able to finally escape it." She took in a deep breath and let it out on a ragged sigh. "At least it seems like you and your siblings are close. I only have my brother, but I swear, he couldn't care less about me or my father. He just wants to live his own life with as few interruptions from his family as possible."

So she was shouldering the whole burden on her own. Well, that would have to change, especially if he had any say in it. "Do you have any other family who could help you to convince your dad to go to rehab? If it's a financial concern, I'd be happy to pay for it, Harper."

"You're a sweet man, but I can't let you do that. And no...there really isn't anyone else capable of convincing him. The only other family I have are my first cousins, but they're from my mom's side of the family, and though they'd do what they could to help, they live on a remote island in Maine, and I'd rather not bother them." She gave him a shrug, looking defeated where the matter of her father was concerned. "Enough about my dad...we should get back to work. Can't be slacking off or my boss might get very angry with me."

Somehow, she managed to push away everything they'd been discussing, and gave him a sultry smile that had him going hard again. "Is that so?"

She flicked her eyebrows up as her eyes sparkled with mischief. "Yep. He even spanks me, if I've been really bad. But shhh...don't tell him...I actually like it—a lot."

"Sweetheart...I think he already knows."

***

After Harper had finally opened up to him, the last thing

Marshall wanted to do was head back to the craziness of the crowds downstairs. "Let's leave the conference for a bit. I think we've seen enough to be inspired, and besides...I already have an idea or two that I'd like to get your opinion on."

He'd been wanting to tell her about his latest idea for a product he felt would be like nothing else on the market, but had wanted to wait for the right time. And now that he felt so close to her, he couldn't help but want to share his idea with her.

Harper shifted in his arms so she could sit back to look at him, her curiosity lighting her eyes so they sparkled with interest. He was glad to see that working allowed her the chance to let go of all her hurt and problems, for a little while, at least. Maybe that was one of the reasons she always seemed so focused on the job. "Now you have me intrigued."

He got to his feet and brought his leather briefcase to the bed, rearranging the numbers on the lock so he could pop it open. He grabbed the file he needed along with his laptop and then, setting aside his case, sat back down on the bed next to her.

"I was thinking of the minute details and physiology of a woman's anatomy when I designed it, since that's what really sets Clio products apart." Flipping through the file, he found the drawings he'd made as a quick mock-up of his idea and handed it to her as he pulled up the schematics for the toy on his laptop. "You see, in addition to a woman's clit and G-spot, there are thousands more nerves in the surrounding tissue of the labia and inner walls of the vagina. And though some vibes add texture and movement to the shaft of a vibrator, it doesn't tend to apply enough pressure on the nerve endings—and there's nothing on the market, that I'm aware of, that addresses the nerves in the labia."

She shook her head, as if not truly believing him. "Really? I guess I've never noticed."

"Maybe a little show-and-tell is in order." Wanting to prove his point, he caught her mouth in an intense kiss as his hand wandered up her thighs to her sweet cunt, still bare from earlier, brushing his fingers over her slick lips, as he broke away from their kiss just enough to be able to speak. "You see, only a very small part of your clit is visible, while the remaining tissue, the corpora cavernosa, runs under the soft folds of your inner labia and around your vagina."

When he massaged the area just right, he had the pleasure of hearing her breath catch and her hips tilt towards him. "Oh...I think I see..."

Her head fell back, gasping when he slipped his fingers inside her for a moment, before going back to massaging her, alternating between the two so that her breath was quickening. "And then...imagine we add further stimulation to your swollen clit."

Pushing her legs apart so that her skirt hiked up her hips, he nestled himself between her legs, continuing to tease her as he had been, but this time letting his tongue stroke her clit, swollen and so ready to set off an explosive orgasm—which is when he pulled away. He gave her a smug smile, ignoring her protests for more.

"Patience, sweet girl." He smeared her juices across her lips, loving that she sucked his fingers into her mouth to lick them clean, the tug going straight to his hard cock. "Because when I do finally let you come, all this waiting will only make your orgasm so much more intense. Not to mention, we still have work to deal with. I want your opinion on my design, especially since I think your new method for providing deeper stimulation could be perfect in this application, given that the tissue we're looking to stimulate lies deeper below the surface."

"You're killing me, Marshall, especially since it's damn sexy when you get all scientific and technical. As for work, I think your idea is downright brilliant. You're right—there's nothing else like this, and it could really be the thing that pushes us even further ahead of the pack." She shifted closer to him, biting her lower lip and giving him a sultry look, her skin flushed from her arousal and her nipples hard against the fabric of her shirt. "Are you sure I can't convince you to do a little more...research? I'll happily be your test subject."

He couldn't help but laugh, slipping his arm around her waist and pulling her close so he could kiss her. "I promise to make you come so many times, you won't be able to stand—but it'll have to wait. I'm hungry, and we have work to do. But you have my word, sweet girl...it'll be well worth the wait."

She gave him a provocative pout, so he couldn't resist catching her plump lip between his teeth and stealing a kiss. "Fine...but, I make no promises to keep my hands off you."

Marshall could already picture her tied to the bed. "Now that sounds like a challenge I'll like."

CHAPTER 16

After they'd gone out for a quick bite, Harper spent the next few hours at Marshall's side as they worked together, discussing his design and tweaking it, so by the time they finished, she was convinced they had a toy unlike any other. Though it looked to an extent like a rabbit vibe, with a long, thick shaft for penetration and a smaller extension to stimulate the clit, it also had a more slender shaft for anal penetration, in addition to a flange at the base, which was designed to stimulate those deep labial nerves.

She found it hard to contain her excitement, her smile stretching from ear to ear. "I can't wait to get the prototype made. I think it's going to be fantastic, Marshall. This is going to blow away the competition."

"You'll be the first to try it—you have my word." Marshall got to his feet, and slowly started unbuttoning his shirt, his sleeves already rolled up to expose the tanned skin on his powerful forearms. But his hands were what held her focus—the hands of a surgeon—as his fingers made quick work of the buttons, knowing just how much they were capable of. Sometimes it seemed as if every touch seemed

CALI MACKAY

to be exact, precise, perfectly planned for giving her maximum pleasure—and then there were the times when he gave in to the passion between them, not thinking at all, just feeding the need between them as their ancient and primal instinct took hold, all thought erased as their bodies took over, feeding their desires.

He slipped his shirt off and tossed it aside, exposing his muscular chest and ripped abs as a thin line of hair led the way. "We should shower...get ready to head out. There's a party we should think about going to."

All she could do was nod, her tongue darting out to lick her lips as he slowly undid his belt and pulled it free of his trousers, doubling it and smacking his palm with it, the simple act making her go wet when he hadn't even touched her. Never before had anyone had such an effect on her. Marshall left her constantly hungry for him, for what he could do to her, and it seemed she'd never get her fill.

With his eyes locked on hers and his gaze stern, he said, "Strip down to nothing, Ms. Jones."

The command in his voice had her immediately complying, as he continued to rid himself of his clothing, though he'd left the belt close by, easily within reach.

"I thought we were going to wait?" She couldn't help but be a little cheeky, but it was probably her defense to feeling so vulnerable. Because he did make her feel vulnerable, damn it.

Somehow, he'd managed to capture her heart, making her feel alive in a way she hadn't felt since before Josh's accident. And even then...this was completely different. It felt so much more intense, and that intensity only ratcheted up her feelings for Marshall and what was at stake, what

156

she could lose if it all went to hell.

It wasn't as though she hadn't tried to push him away, for all the good it did. And now...well, now, she was in deep, unable to resist him, and willing to play whatever games he wanted. But there was more to it than just the physical attraction. Truth was, she was falling for him, even if she knew she shouldn't, her longtime crush turning into something so much more.

"Sweet girl—you're not going to come until I'm ready to let you. However, that doesn't mean I won't be teasing you all night long—nor does it mean that I won't be coming." Now standing naked before her, he wrapped his hand around his erection, and with smoky eyes locked on hers, he stroked himself, thrusting his hard cock through his fist as he watched her undress, her clothes tossed haphazardly on the floor. "As sexy and gorgeous as you are, there's no way I'll be able to last the whole night without having you."

"That's not fair, now is it?" Down to just her panties, she knelt on the bed and, running her fingers over the lace, she hooked the edge onto her thumbs and slowly shimmied them down over her hips and tossed them off, aiming for sexy, and hoping she didn't look like a fool. It'd been too long since she last did anything like this, and it was hard not to feel self-conscious about it.

"Fair?" He gave her a sexy laugh. "I promise, it'll be more than fair when I have you coming so many times, you don't remember anyone's name but mine."

"And if I come anyway? What then?" Just to prove her point, she let her hand slowly slip down over the curve of her belly to her clit as she bit her lower lip with a needy groan, cupping her breast with her other hand and pinching her nipple so she felt it shoot right through to her core.

Worked up as she was from him teasing her earlier, coming would not be a problem.

"Harper...you're being a very bad girl." And yet, he hadn't stopped stroking himself, his hips thrusting his cock through his fist as he took a step closer to her.

"What are you going to do about it, Marshall?" She could see the jewel of pre-cum glistening on the tip, stoking her need for him so her pace quickened, her fingers gliding over her clit and slipping inside her. "Because whatever it is, you better hurry...'cause I'm going to...come..."

She was so close, the tension building inside her as every nerve came alive—but then Marshall closed the distance between them, and grabbed her wrist, pulling her hand away from her clit, before taking her by the waist and flipping her onto all fours. Before she knew it, he was slapping her ass, the burning sting blossoming over her skin when he thrust into her bare, his balls hitting her already swollen and sensitive clit.

"Mine." He growled the word in her ear, sending a needy shiver through her as his muscular chest pressed to her back, his hand gently squeezing around her throat, his thrusts hard enough to have her repositioning her arms to brace herself. "Say it, Harper...tell me that you're mine and no one else's."

In that moment, with him taking her rough and hard, her body linked to his, skin to skin, she realized that somewhere along the way he'd claimed not only her body but was well on his way to claiming her heart as well. Suddenly, she found that all pretenses were gone, and there was no point in denying how she felt about him. "I'm yours, Marshall...I don't want anyone but you."

"All mine—just like I'm yours, Harper." His thrusts filled her, pushing her closer and closer to her orgasm, every nerve in her body thrumming with sexual tension, even as she tried to hold back.

"I'm so close...please...I can't..." She was going to come, even though he'd told her not to.

"Don't do it, sweet girl." Yet his pace was relentless and he had her teetering on the edge. He pulled out of her as she cried out in protest, his absence leaving her feeling so empty and desperate for him. "Lie back on the pillows and grab the headboard."

She did as he asked, wondering what was to come next. Watching him with eager anticipation, he grabbed the bag from the convention and emptied all the promo products onto the mattress, a sundry of sex toys, lubes, and pamphlets spilling across the comforter. When she spoke, it was impossible to keep the sliver of panic—or was it excitement—from her voice. "Marshall..."

"Let's see what we have here, shall we?" The humor and mischief in his eye had her squirming in her spot, her grip on the headboard tightening. "What about this, sweetness?"

He held up a roll that looked like duct tape with a logo running along its length—but she knew better. It was bondage tape, so he could tie her up anyway he wanted, since the tape would only stick to itself. The thought of being at his mercy—the thought of the things he could do to her, the pleasure he could give her, only made her want him all the more, especially when he looked so damn sexy with his hair disheveled and mischief in his eyes, not to mention his long, hard cock. "Anything you want, Marshall."

His eyebrows perked up in question with a tilt of his head, taking her in as if trying to figure out if she was serious. He cupped her face in his large hand, his touch warm and his skin just a little rough, and then ran his thumb over her lips, her pulse racing as she sucked in a breath and her eyes fluttered shut.

"Sweet girl...open your eyes and look at me." She did as he asked, her heart catching as if she was seeing him for the first time, a pang in her chest as she felt herself fall head over heels in love with him. "Do you trust me? Because none of this is any fun if you don't trust me and it doesn't give you pleasure."

There was no pause as she answered, for there was no doubt in her heart or head. "I trust you completely, Marshall."

She just hoped he felt the same way about her, and wouldn't break her heart.

Supporting himself with a hand on the headboard, he leaned in and kissed her, his mouth catching hers in a long, tender kiss that flamed her need for him, her body physically aching from wanting him so badly. And when he bit her lip, it felt like it was a live wire straight to her clit, and she swore, it was nearly enough to have her coming right there, her legs squeezing together in the hope of finding some relief.

Kneeling by her side, he grabbed his cock and brushed it against her lips, smearing the pre-cum as her tongue darted out to lick him. But when she tried to sit forward to take her into his mouth, he fisted her hair and gently pulled her head back, ignoring her needy cries. "I set the pace, Harper. Am I clear?" When she nodded, he continued. "Do you have a safe word you like to use?"

PASSION

"No…I guess I've never needed one before."

What was she getting herself into?

CHAPTER 17

F **uck...Marshall was** so hard, but he knew he'd have to hold back and ease Harper into things, especially if she hadn't experimented much. And yet, he loved that she was so willing to trust him, to let him do what he wanted and to try new things. "Then let's pick a safe word — just in case you need it. Some people use 'red' — as in stop."

She nodded, her breaths shallow and skin flushed with arousal, as he slowly stroked himself, unable to resist when she looked so gorgeous. "I can remember that."

Grabbing a length of the bondage tape, he tied her delicate wrists together, before binding them to the bed, her nipples hard and her body stretched tight so that her breasts sat perky and high as if in offering. Unable to resist, he let his fingers trail over her skin, between her breasts, pausing to tease and pinch her nipples erect, giving them a tug and rolling them between his finger and thumb. She bit back a groan, her hips rocking towards him, begging for his touch, when he grabbed a pair of nipple clamps, loving how her eyes went wide and her breath quickened at the sight of them.

"Just a bit of pressure to heighten everything. It'll be

okay, love—and you have your safe word if it gets to be too much." He attached the flat clip to her nipples and tightened the screws to apply just enough pressure to arouse without being too intense, a silver chain dangling between the two.

Slipping his finger down between her breasts, he hooked the chain and gave it a bit of a tug to make sure the clamps wouldn't come loose and to judge her reaction to them. Her back arched and her hips rocked towards him in response as she bit her bottom lip to hold back a needy whimper. "Marshall...I'm begging you to let me come. Please...I'll do anything."

"Hush... Patience, sweet girl." When he let his fingers drift down over the curves of her belly to her sex, he knew just how wet he'd find her. Slipping through her delicate folds, he slowly thrust his fingers into her. "Oh, babe...you're so ready for me..."

She let out a strangled cry when he continued to finger fuck her, pulling his fingers out and along her lips before plunging them back in oh so slowly, teasing her everywhere but her clit. He knew she was teetering on the edge of coming and didn't want to push her over just yet. "Please, Marshall...I'm so close...so fucking close..."

"I know, sweetheart...but it'll be so much better when you do finally come." He doubted she'd last the whole night, and that was fine. By the time she did orgasm, he had no doubt it'd be intense. After all she'd been through the last three years, he wanted to give her pleasure unlike anything she'd ever experienced before.

Straddling her chest, he leaned over her, propping himself up with a hand on the headboard, which put him in the perfect position to claim her mouth. Grabbing his cock, he slipped it across her lips, her mouth falling open as she leaned forward and ran her tongue over the head of his cock before wrapping her lips around his girth.

She was so fucking gorgeous with his cock slipping into her sweet mouth as she sucked him eagerly. He thrust forward, forcing her to take more of him with each pass, though with the pace she was setting, he knew he wouldn't last. Knotting his hand through her hair, he fisted it, taking control so she could no longer move forward and he could take things nice and slow.

"That feels so good, Harper... so fucking good..." His hips rocked towards her as he watched her take all of him, her plump lips wrapped around his cock as her tongue teased him and her needy moans vibrated against his shaft. He wanted it to last, but he swore it was impossible when it felt so fucking amazing. His pace started to pick up, despite his best intentions, the energy and tension building at the base of his cock until he could take little more and was coming undone; her blue eyes locked on his, leaving him unable to hide the effect she had on him.

"Fuck, Harper..." His orgasm tore through him as he shot his cum down her throat, his cock pulsing as she continued to suck him, swallowing everything he had to give her until he was finally spent, his body tense with the last tremors of his orgasm, until he was finally able to pull free of that gorgeous mouth of hers. "Sweet girl...I swear, I could so easily fall in love with you."

With pursed lips, she looked at him as if she was trying to figure out if he actually meant what he'd said, before giving a shake of her head, clearly dismissing it. "That's just post-orgasmic stupidity talking. But I swear, Marshall—if you don't let me come soon, that'll be the last time I suck you off."

He couldn't help but laugh, stealing a lingering kiss and giving her nipple clamps a tug, loving it when she groaned. "Though I'm sure you don't mean such cruel words, I'm not one to take risks, especially when it comes to your lips wrapped around my cock. If you want to come, then I'll make you come. Just remember...you're the one who asked for it."

"What's that supposed to mean?" Though she sounded a little panicked, he couldn't help but laugh and kiss her again, before he trailed kisses over the curves of her belly, shifting down and nestling himself between her legs.

"It means I'm going to make you come so many times, you'll be weak-kneed for days." And he was going to love every minute of it. "Anything off-limits, sweet girl? And is there anything you've ever been curious about and wanted to try?"

She cringed, clearly not comfortable with the discussion, even if she'd just had his cock in her mouth. "Can't we just...do this? You always want to discuss things."

He cupped her cheek, his touch gentle. "If it means it'll get you what you want, what you need, then why not? I won't judge you, Harper. But...I get it. Sometimes it's not easy to ask for what you want."

"Please, Marshall...just make me come. That's all I want, and you're killing me." Her hips shifted and squirmed in her desperation, and open as she was to him, he could see just how wet she was from sucking him off.

But first, he wanted to make sure he pushed her as close to the edge as he could without actually pushing her over. He grabbed a butt plug out of the pile and slipped it against her slick lips, dipping it inside her to get it slick, before he pressed it to the bud of her ass, slowly easing it in.

"There you go, sweetheart...just relax, and push back against it." She bit her bottom lip, her eyes fluttering shut as she did what he asked, so the plug slid in and was now firmly seated. He knew it would intensify everything he did to her, and when he ran his fingers over her slick heat and plunged them deep inside her sweet cunt, her gasp came as no surprise. Slowly, he slipped two fingers in and out of her, curling them against the tender bundle of nerves as her body tightened around his fingers, his pace increasing until she was coming, crying out his name.

With her orgasm still crashing through her, he sucked her clit into his mouth, flicking and teasing it with his tongue as he continued to thrust into her, lapping at her as he pulled her first orgasm into the next, one building on the other as she gasped and quivered in his arms, her legs tightening around his shoulders as she bucked against him. But he didn't let up...not until she rode out the last waves of her orgasm. Only then did he slow his attentions, her hurried gasps of breath finally slowing as her body started to relax.

He trailed kisses down the inside of her thigh to her knee, her skin silky soft. Each kiss sent another quiver through her, though he was nowhere near done with her, his cock hard once again and aching to have her. He ran the head of his cock up against her clit and down to her slit, teasing her, as she rocked her hips against him, though he wasn't ready to plunge into her just yet. "How are you doing, sweetheart?"

"I swear, when this is all over, I'm going to murder you— or worship at your feet. I haven't decided yet." Her hands tightened around the headboard as if she were trying to keep herself from drifting away. "You make me crazy, Marshall."

"That's what I like to hear." He leaned forward and caught her mouth in a hard kiss, his tongue dancing over hers as he thrust his cock into her slick heat, burying himself deep. She was so fucking tight, especially when the plug was vying for what little space there was.

Hooking her legs onto his shoulders, he thrust into her with deep, driving strokes, knowing that the position she was now in meant that his cock would not only hit her G-spot, but he'd also grind against her clit. His pace quickened as he took her with hard, punishing strokes, swallowing her needy cries as he claimed her body once more and pushed her towards yet another orgasm.

When he bit her neck, it was just what was needed to have her coming again, though this time she was nearly frantic with it, crying out his name as her body trembled and shook with the waves of her orgasm. He slowed his thrusts, covering her face in gentle kisses until her breathing finally slowed, though he swore he didn't think his heart would ever recover.

"Sunshine..." Fighting the need to come, he slowly pulled free of her, and then, kneeling between her legs, he removed the nipple clamps, silencing her cries by gently sucking her nipples into his mouth, one and then the other, his tongue swirling around them, hoping to turn the flicker of pain to pleasure. "Do you have one more for me, love? I want you to come one last time."

He knew he was asking a lot of her, but he'd never felt so close to anyone before. Certainly not Claire, who didn't have a passionate bone in her body once she'd gotten what she wanted.

"I don't know if I can, Marshall...it's been so intense..."
And yet the way she looked at him, so willing to please him,
so willing to take all that he could give her, he knew he had
the answer, even if she didn't yet know she was capable of
it.

"You have your safe word. Okay? Use it if you want me
to stop at any point." Reaching up, he undid her arms,
rubbing them carefully to get the blood moving again,
before he brought them to his lips, kissing one wrist and
then the other. Running his hands down her legs, he pushed
her knees towards her chest, and slowly pulled the plug free
of her body. "There you go... Just once more, Harper..."

He grabbed a packet of lube, tore it open and applied it
to his cock as he knelt before her, desperate to have
everything she could offer him. Hooking her legs up over his
shoulders, he scooped her up into his arms as she wrapped
them around his neck and held onto him and he slowly
lowered her onto his slick cock, the bud of her ass opening
for him as he breached the tight ring of muscle.

She was completely at his mercy in this position, as he
carefully eased himself into her, taking things as slow as he
could, in order to make sure he gave her body enough time
to adjust. "You okay, love?"

"It's intense, but...wow. Yeah...I'm fine...more than
fine..." And then she was kissing him hungrily, frantically,
urging him on as he gripped her waist, slowly lifting and
lowering her onto his hard length.

She was so incredibly tight, and it felt so fucking good, he
swore he'd never felt anything like it. "Bloody hell,
Harper...you feel amazing."

Her mouth was on his once more in response, his tongue

finding hers in a heated dance as his pace quickened, driving himself deep inside her and claiming her once more. He was so fucking close to coming, the tension thrummed inside his body like he was trying to hold back a summer storm, taking them both deeper, harder, until she was crying out once more as she came in his arms, his own orgasm tearing through him with those final thrusts, his cock pulsing deep inside her ass as he filled her with his hot cum, his heart and soul hers.

"Fuck, Harper...I swear I'm in love with you." He lowered her to the mattress and cradled her to his body, kissing her face sweetly as his cock slipped free of her body and his cum spilled out of her ass and down onto her thighs. "Are you okay?"

Her body shuddered in his arms as she burrowed deep in his embrace, making him worry. He knew he should have kept his mouth shut, but fuck...she was making his head spin.

With a ragged breath, she kissed his neck, pressing her lips to the pulse on his neck, before returning her head to his chest. "I think I love you too, Marshall...though I also think too many orgasms have left us brain dead, and clearly not thinking straight."

He couldn't help but smile as he kissed the top of her head. She may be right, but at that moment, he didn't care. She was his, and nothing had ever felt so right. "Just so we're clear, there's no way I'm ever giving you up, sweet girl."

CHAPTER 18

Harper was relieved that Marshall had decided to skip the party, though it was a day later and she still couldn't walk without her legs wanting to wobble and give out from under her as she wove through the crowds of the conference. Marshall was downright amazing, and it was a good thing they'd decided to keep this thing of theirs going once they got back home.

Marshall was spoiling her, and she didn't think she'd ever be able to give up the way he made love to her all night long, or waking in his arms each morning. It'd been years since she'd been this happy and content, but she also knew how easy it could all get taken away. It's not as though their lives weren't complicated. Any number of things could derail their budding relationship, even if they wanted it all to work out, and the thought of losing him—just like she'd lost Josh—was like a thorn in her heart.

"You okay, sweetness?" With a strong arm around her waist, Marshall pulled her to him and pressed a kiss to her temple, the gesture so sweet and romantic, she couldn't help but lean into him, a smile slipping onto her lips. "It looks like you're thinking too hard."

"Not anymore." Pushing aside her worries, she turned in to him, nestling herself in his warm embrace so she could nip at his neck, even as the people swirled around them in the lobby of the hotel.

He groaned in response, letting his hands slip from her waist down to her ass, hauling her body against his, so it was impossible for her to ignore his hard length. "You make it so I can't think of anything but you."

"Is that a bad thing?" She pulled away just enough to look up at him with a sultry smile, loving that he made her feel so damn sexy—and in a way no other man had ever made her feel. What was between them suddenly felt all-consuming, and she didn't ever want it to end.

"Only if you don't feel the same way, sunshine." There was an expectant look in his eyes, as if he was worried about how she truly felt about him—and it killed her that Claire had left him uneasy about trusting others' emotions.

Hating that he'd been so hurt, she cupped his cheek, his stubble rough against the palm of her hand, and kissed him, slow and sweet, her lips lingering on his. "I love you, Marshall—and those aren't words I speak easily."

He let out a deep breath as if he'd been holding onto it, and then gave her a crooked smile. "Good—because I've fallen for you hard, Harper. From the moment I first laid eyes on you."

***

Harper checked the scheduled events for the day, and was relieved that things looked to be winding down some. "Would you hate me if I abandoned you and headed back to the room? I haven't checked email in days, and I wanted to work on your vibe idea. Maybe incorporate the details we'd discussed and come up with a new schematic."

"Go on ahead without me. I'm on that panel in another hour, so I'll be tied up with that anyway. I don't think I sent you the schematics, so just grab them off my laptop and my briefcase, okay?" He pulled out a pen and paper and jotted down a few things before handing it to her. "My passwords. If you have any problems, just call me."

"Marshall…I really don't want to have access to your passwords, especially with everything that's going on." She'd be devastated if their competitors got their hands on these most recent designs—but she also didn't want to have any reason for him to doubt her loyalty.

"I trust you, Harper, and if it makes you feel any better, I'll change my passwords later. But I know you're not going to snoop around in my stuff, and frankly, I have nothing to hide." He cupped the back of her neck and pulled her close, his masculine scent filling her head so she ached for him to take her once more, knowing she'd never get her fill of him now that he'd awakened that part of her. And then he kissed her, his mouth lingering on hers, clearly not caring that they were in a room full of people. His kisses trailed off though he kept her close, his cheek brushing hers, making her want to drag him back up to their room, even if she was still deliciously sore from their adventures. "I promise not to be too long."

Happiness bubbled inside her chest—something she hadn't felt in a very long time. Not since Josh, though what she had with Marshall felt different in so many ways. Though she'd loved Josh and they'd been great together before his accident, she felt like she could be more open with Marshall, especially when it came to being intimate— even if she still had a hard time getting it all out there.

She gave him a teasing smile and sidled up against his tall, muscular form, desperate to have him claim her once more. "I'll be waiting, though take too long, and I might start without you."

She swore he almost looked proud of her, his eyes alight as he cupped her cheek. "That's what I like to hear. I fucking love it that you're getting to be more comfortable with me—and with yourself, your body. It makes me a happy man, Ms. Harper Jones."

That fact that her happiness and gratification meant so much to him...that it wasn't just about his pleasure, but hers—maybe even more so—went straight to her heart. And if she'd been holding back on the feelings she had for him, that was no longer the case, for he'd claimed not only her body, but her heart and soul. "You're a rare man, Marshall."

With a final kiss goodbye, she headed up to their room, grabbed her cell phone, and called her dad. It rang and rang, but ended up going to voicemail. She tried again, telling herself not to panic. Though he seldom went anywhere anymore, he could be out in the garden or taking a shower. Voicemail again. Crap.

She called Brian next, hoping her brother could set her mind at ease. At least he answered his phone, though she could already tell he was annoyed with her. "Before you even ask, Dad's fine."

Harper felt the knot in her chest loosen as relief washed over her. "So, you went by there today to check on him?"

"I spoke with him this morning, and went by there yesterday. He's fine, Harper. I swear, I think you forget that he's a grown man."

"I haven't forgotten, Brian. But until he gets the help he needs, he needs us to be there for him. We need to remind him that it's worth getting up to face another day." She hated to think of it, but she knew how close her father was to letting the darkness take him, and she couldn't bear the thought of losing him. "You'll go by there and check on him, right?"

"Yeah...as soon as I wrap up with work. But, fuck, Harper..." He let out a sigh. "Never mind. Enjoy London, okay?"

At least he was going to check in on their dad, though she was annoyed that she couldn't even hand the reins over to Brian for just a few days without having him bitch and moan.

Knowing work would help her forget how frustrated she was with her brother, she grabbed Marshall's laptop and briefcase and, after punching in his passcodes, found the files and papers she was looking for. Looking over the design for Marshall's vibe, a thrum of excitement bubbled up inside her. It was brilliant. Intuitive too, since it could sense how and when the woman tensed so it could increase or decrease the intensity and type of vibrations. It would even have a variety of different settings, like "tease" for a slow build to an incredible orgasm, or "multiples" for an intense experience that would have you coming over and over again.

She spent the next few hours working on the design and figuring out the details of the internal components and how they'd come together in such a compact design. Though she was happy working, her focus still strayed to Marshall, leaving her to wonder how she'd gone and fallen for him. Granted, they'd been flirting around Clio since she got there nine months earlier, but what they were now doing was a huge leap from chitchat and sexy glances over by the coffee and donuts—and it was exactly what she needed.

Marshall made her happier than she'd been in a very long time, and though she still felt guilty about moving on when Josh was clearly having a much harder time of it, she was tired of letting life pass her by, and living in the past. She, of all people, should know better, when she'd seen the devastating effects holding onto the past had on her father. It'd been just over a decade since her mother's death, and he still hadn't gotten over it.

When her phone buzzed with an incoming message, her stomach fluttered with excitement and her pulse raced as her thoughts immediately went to Marshall—except that it wasn't him. Caught up in the fun she'd been having with him, she'd completely forgotten that she was supposed to have dinner with Ben, and he wanted to make sure they were still on. Crap.

She'd much rather spend the evening with Marshall and all that entailed, yet she hadn't seen Ben in ages and the last thing she wanted to become was a clingy girlfriend who had to spend every waking moment by her man's side. Maybe Marshall would join them? After all, it wasn't like it was a date. Just dinner between friends. And as star-struck as Ben had been with Marshall, she didn't think Ben would mind.

Yet she knew Ben was hoping for a little more than just dinner, and she wasn't sure she wanted to encourage him or make him think there was hope for a hookup when things were just starting to get serious with Marshall. Maybe skipping dinner and grabbing a cup of coffee would be a better option.

She texted him back, asking if he was free for a quick caffeine break, with apologies for having to skip out on dinner. Perfect—he'd meet her in the hotel lobby in half an hour. Just enough time for her to wrap up the last of her notes.

Quickly, she freshened up, and headed down to the lobby, spotting Ben easily, despite the crowds, since he stood several inches above most men in the room and was beyond cute, in a sexy geek kind of way, with his glasses and mussed-up hair. His smile lit up his face when he saw her approaching.

"Hey, you." Ben pulled her into a big hug and gave her a quick peck on the lips, though it was too brief to address, and she didn't want to make an issue out of something innocent or casual. "It's been too long, Harper."

"I'm just glad we could do this. Sorry about dinner, but things are crazy. I'm still trying to get work done around all this convention stuff." When she slipped out of his arms, his hand slipped to the small of her back as he steered her through the crowds in the hotel lobby towards one of the cafés. Though it was a small gesture, it immediately reminded her of Marshall, her heart missing him with a tiny pang, and making her feel silly that she could miss someone she hadn't seen for mere hours.

"Has Dr. Foley been keeping you busy then?" They somehow managed to find a loveseat and table being vacated and Ben quickly snagged it before anyone else could steal it from them. It was crammed into the far corner of the café, and cozier than she'd like, but as crowded as the place was with the convention attendees, she was lucky she hadn't ended up in Ben's lap.

"You know what it's like—things are always busy. But I

hadn't originally planned to come to this event, so I'm still trying to get some work done. Luckily, Marshall hasn't needed too much from me for the convention, so I've been able to stay focused on our project." She still couldn't believe Marshall was having her help him with the design of his most innovative product yet—and he'd be incorporating her new technology into it.

"Look at your eyes light up, Harper." Ben gave her a flirty smile and shifted in on the sofa so they were facing each other. "That must be one hell of a design he has you working on. Don't suppose you want to tell me more about it?"

"No offense, but no way." She knew Ben was joking and likely didn't know that Clio's designs may have been stolen by Titan, but there wasn't a chance in hell that she'd be saying a single word about it. "Marshall's a nice guy, but stuff like that gets people fired."

"Honestly, I was kidding. It's the same over where I work, though they're not as nice about it." They took a moment to place their order with the waitress who was weaving between the tables. "Actually...that's one of the reasons I wanted to talk to you. I was thinking I might start up my own company, and wanted to know if you'd like to join me. I miss New England and want to head back there. California's nice, but I miss the change of seasons—among other things."

That really wasn't what she'd expected at all. "So you're going to put together a start-up? Do you have the capital to do that sort of thing?"

"I found a willing investor who's got enough cash set aside to get us started." He reached over and gave her hand a squeeze. "Come on, Harper. You know it'd be so much fun. Just like old times, with the two of us in the lab together. And just think of the money we could make when it takes off—which you know it would."

"It sounds great, Ben. And I'll love having you close by again, but…I can't." It felt like she'd be betraying Marshall. "I'm happy working at Clio, and with my dad…I can't risk my finances, since I send a good chunk of my paycheck his way to pay his bills."

"Just do me a favor and think about it. I've put together a packet for you—just in case you want to give it a little more thought." Ben dug around in his messenger bag and pulled out a stapled packet of papers, handing them to her. "Sorry it's so basic, but I didn't realize you'd be here. I was going to get in touch once I got back and put things into motion. I know you've got your concerns, but this sort of opportunity doesn't happen too often, and I don't want you to miss out on it. Not to mention, there's a sign-on bonus, stock options—and did I mention how much fun we'd have working together?"

She flicked through the packet just out of curiosity, and she had to say she was damn impressed. "Wow…this is…generous."

"Exactly. Just promise me you'll go through it and really give it some thought before you give me your final answer."

CHAPTER 19

As the moderator asked if there were any questions for the panelists, Marshall hoped they'd ignore Claire, who was sitting in the front row and had her hand raised. Somehow he'd managed to ignore her during the discussion, and it looked like he might escape without her getting the chance to ambush him as the moderator picked one person after another. Until they announced they'd take one last question.

Claire stood up and pinned him with a triumphant glare and smug smile as she stood up and started to ask her question—not that he was hanging around. He leaned over towards the moderator, made an excuse, and slipped away out the side door. Life was too short to continue to subject himself to Claire's insanity and bitchiness.

Though he'd always wanted a child, he still couldn't believe Claire was pregnant. Especially when she'd always been so careful about making sure he wore a condom, not wanting to subject her body to the Pill on the off chance she put on an extra pound or two—and not wanting to risk getting pregnant. Hell...he'd never even been with his own wife skin to skin. So for her to suddenly be pregnant? He just wasn't buying it. And it killed him that what should be a happy occasion was instead turned into a manipulative mess.

His phone vibrated in his pocket, pulling him from his thoughts. Keane… "Hey. How's it going over there?"

"Busy." There was a long pause on the line before Keane continued. "Listen…I'm working with the Rykers' security firm like you recommended, and we've made a bit of headway on who might be behind the thefts."

"Who?" Marshall couldn't believe they were finally getting somewhere with it. Once he'd spoken to Quinn Ryker about the problems they were having at Clio, Quinn had recommended Gabe's fiancée, Hadley, and her security firm—and it looked like it'd been the right move.

"We've narrowed it down to someone on the engineering team—I have her name here somewhere. Harper Jones."

It was like a knife to his heart, leaving Marshall stunned and shattered with disbelief.

"It can't be, Keane. I know her, and she wouldn't do something like this. No fucking way." It just couldn't be. Marshall refused to believe Harper had anything to do with this mess. There was no way she could be the mole. "What proof do you have?"

"Nothing concrete, but there's an awful lot pointing in her direction. Her work computer had accessed files she shouldn't have been looking at." Keane let out a weary sigh. "I know she's there at the conference with you, Marshall. Are you sleeping with her?"

Fucking hell. "Yeah, I am. But I swear, Keane…there's got to be a reasonable explanation. A lot of the computers in her department have multiple users on them."

"I know. Which is why we're looking into it further. But, Marshall...I'm not sure letting her get close to you is a good idea." After another long pause that made him want to reach through the phone and shake his brother, Keane finally continued. "There's more. Locked away in her desk drawer were copies of plans she shouldn't have had—and there was correspondence to a rival company. Titan."

"Keep me updated, Keane. But I need to know for sure. Not just half-assed suspicions, okay?" Anger, hurt, and doubt—about whether she could be guilty, about whether what was between them was real—all rivaled with each other as Marshall hung up with his brother and stepped onto the elevator, fighting the urge to put his fist through the wall.

He let himself into their room, still not quite sure what he'd say to her. Not that it mattered, since she wasn't even there. Where the hell was she? Both their laptops, along with his briefcase, were still on the bed—and he'd given her his password.

Fuck...he hated to think the worst and couldn't imagine that she was involved. Yet her friend worked for Titan. Keane had narrowed down the mole to someone in Harper's department at a bare minimum, and though it was hard to know when exactly the thefts had started, it wasn't that far off from when Harper came to work for Clio. And now? She'd said she'd wanted to come back to the room so she could get some work done, and yet she wasn't here, even if she'd clearly accessed his files.

She'd mentioned her father had problems and she was hoping to get him help. Were things bad enough that she was forced to do things that may be out of character for her out of sheer desperation? Or was the issue something bigger, like gambling, and she just hadn't told him about it?

He hated to do it, but he had to. Carefully, he went through her briefcase and her luggage, trying not to disturb anything, and then turned his attention to her laptop, though she had it password protected, and he was damned if he could figure out how to get past it.

Needing a drink, he grabbed himself a whiskey and knocked it back, getting himself another before he grabbed a seat so he could wait for her while attempting to sort through his racing thoughts. It couldn't be Harper. He couldn't bear to think of her being guilty of doing such a thing—and worse, he couldn't bear to think that what was between them had been nothing more than a deliberate manipulation. It fucking killed him, his heart strangled by his heartache, as he did his best to push away the thought that she was the mole.

Let it be anyone but her...

He was on his fourth whiskey and in a foul mood by the time she showed up, a smile lighting her face when she saw him. "Hey...when did you get back? You should have texted me."

She put down her handbag, and slipped some folded papers she was holding into her purse, before closing the distance between them to sit on his lap with her arms around his neck and a smile on her lips. Her mere presence melted away some of his doubts about her, and when she kissed him, he couldn't help but kiss her back, his fingers sinking into her hair as she shifted to straddle him. By the time he managed to break away from their kiss, his breathing was heavy and his head was spinning. "I missed you, Harper."

She pulled back to look at him, worry darkening her eyes and creasing her brow. "Hey...you okay? What's happened?"

"Where were you, sunshine?" He hated asking like he was some sort of jealous dick of a boyfriend. And maybe he was. But given everything that was going on, he wanted answers.

Her eyes narrowed just a little as if wondering why the hell he was grilling her like some sort of possessive asshole, although she answered him anyway. "Ben texted to see if I was still up for dinner, but I figured I'd rather spend the evening with you, so I met with him for coffee instead, since I needed the caffeine and it'd get me off the hook for meeting with him later. Why? What's going on? You look totally out of sorts, not to mention just a little drunk."

So she'd been with Ben. But was it really just to catch up quickly over a caffeine boost? Marshall couldn't help but wonder if she'd found the files she needed on his laptop and was handing them over, knowing he'd be busy with his panel and the conference. Fuck, but he hated himself for thinking it of her, even if he had a right to think it.

"I'm sorry...I'm being an ass." Which was nothing but the truth. "Did you have a good time, at least?"

"Yeah...I suppose. It was nice to see him again, since it'd been awhile, but...it was just coffee." She gave him a shrug and slipped her arms around his neck, concern still lining her face. "Marshall...what's going on? You can talk to me, you know."

Could he? He just didn't know anymore. But one thing was certain—he needed to get a grip and convince her that everything was fine, until he knew otherwise. Because if it turned out to be someone other than Harper—and he sure as hell hoped it was—then the last thing he wanted was to ruin things between them.

Marshall had meant it when he'd told her he was falling in love with her, and though he knew it'd happened quickly, he didn't care. He loved her. There was no changing that. Which was why he needed to keep Keane's suspicions to himself. And if it did turn out to be her, he'd be nothing short of devastated, not to mention it'd have him questioning his judgment when it came to women.

The mess with Claire was bad enough. He didn't need to add another stupid mistake to it, to really make him feel like a gullible idiot. So he'd do his best to pretend there was nothing truly wrong, even if it felt like the walls were crashing in on him.

"My brother called about some business stuff, and it's a pain in the ass trying to deal with certain things when I'm not there in person. But there's nothing to worry about, and I'm sorry if it put me in a shitty mood." When she bent her head to his, he stole a kiss, the physical connection between them seemingly the only thing that could soothe and distract him from his troubles.

"Just promise me you'll talk to me if it gets worse or it becomes too much." She played with his silk tie before loosening it. "I meant it when I said I loved you, Marshall, and I'm here if you need me. No matter what."

He wanted to believe her—and so he did—until he couldn't do otherwise.

"I do love you, Harper...more than you know." He wanted to trust her, wanted things to go back to how they'd been just hours ago, when, no matter what problems they were dealing with, Harper was still the sunshine on a dark and miserable day. So how the hell could he just pretend that everything was normal between them?

She pursed her lips, still looking worried, and then bit her bottom lip. "Do you need to fly back to Portmore? I can stay behind and handle whatever business you have left to wrap up, if that'll help."

He hated that instead of seeing the gesture as one of offered help, he was instead left wondering if she was offering to stay behind so she could meet up with Ben again.

Fuck...what the hell was he doing?

Doing his best, he let go of the tension knotting his muscles and managed a smile, cupping her face as he tried to see her once more as the person he'd fallen in love with. "I appreciate the offer, and though it might be a good idea to head back home, there's nothing I'd need you to stay behind for. I'll have them get the jet ready for tomorrow, if that's okay with you."

"Yeah...of course. Although you really do have me worried about you, Marshall." At least her concern seemed genuine—which made him feel like an ass for questioning why she was with him. "This doesn't have to do with your ex, does it? Or...the baby?"

"No. Though Claire keeps showing up everywhere I'm at, I've managed to avoid talking to her." Maybe if he told her a portion of the truth, it'd allow him to judge her reaction. "I don't remember if I told you, but I have my brother working with a security company to try to narrow down who the mole is."

"Well, that's good. Have they figured out who it is?" Harper didn't seem worried, at least. That had to mean something—unless she was a half decent actress. Given that he didn't want to think she was involved, could he really trust his judgment when it came to her?

"They're getting closer, but nothing concrete yet." He didn't want to tell her that they'd narrowed it down to her department. But why? So she wouldn't get suspicious and cover her tracks? It was fucking insane, and it pissed him off to no end that he was having to analyze every look, every touch, every word out of her mouth.

"I still can't believe someone at Clio would do that, but...maybe you need to relax—let your brother deal with it for now. You have me worried about you." Trailing kisses and bites from his ear to his neck, she slipped her hands down his chest and started undoing the buttons of his shirt. "We haven't used that massive tub yet...maybe a bath— among other things—would help to relax you."

"Maybe." There was one thing he wanted to do first, though. Doing his best to put on a good face to keep her from worrying, he shifted her off his lap and got up, stealing a quick kiss before turning her around and playfully slapping her ass. "Why don't you draw the bath and get started, and I'll join you in just a bit. I have a few things I need to take care of first. And don't forget to grab a vibe, Ms. Jones. I do believe you've been slacking on your research."

She shook her head as she laughed. "That space has been occupied by your hard cock almost exclusively since we got here, so if it's anyone's fault that I'm slacking in my duties, it's yours."

And just like that, their little bit of banter had his heart hitching, leaving him to wonder how he could possibly suspect her. Tangling his fingers in her hair, he hauled her to him for a kiss, claiming her mouth once more, as her soft curves pressed against his body, his hard cock trapped between them, desperately searching her out. His tongue danced over hers as her hands fisted his shirt and he swallowed her needy moans, so he couldn't think of anything but what was between them. By the time their kiss came to an end, he couldn't think straight. Taking a deep breath, he forced himself to focus and try to keep a clear head.

"Off with you, sweet girl. By the time I slip into the hot water next to your naked body, I want you to be able to give me a full report." He grabbed his favorite of the vibes they manufactured and handed it to her, loving that she still blushed even after all they'd done together.

"You really are a brat, Marshall." And then with a sway of her hips and a flirty glance over her shoulder, she headed off, leaving him behind to try to figure out what the hell he was going to do.

Grabbing his cell, he called his brother. "Keane...please fucking tell me you have more news. This is killing me."

"We're still zeroing in on things, but...fuck, man...it's not looking good. Everything points to Harper Jones, though I'm trying to make sure that someone else isn't setting her up to take the fall."

"How far back does the evidence go?" Marshall needed to know when this all started. Ben had recommended she apply for the job at Clio, but was it to get her into the company so she could steal their designs, or was it something more recent?

"We've only found more recent stuff, to be honest, but that's not necessarily conclusive of anything. We may not have uncovered the evidence yet or she may have been doing a better job of covering her tracks early on." Keane let out a weary breath. "I'm sorry, Marshall. I really am. I know you've been through a lot as of late, and this is just one more headache."

"I'm heading back to Portmore tomorrow. We'll deal with this then, though if you find anything else, let me know." He hung up with Keane, pacing the floor as he tried yet again to slow his racing thoughts.

When he saw the folded papers sticking out of Harper's purse, he knew he had to have a look, even if he felt like a shit for doing it. Things were dire, and he had to find out if she was the mole. Given that she'd been out with Ben, he needed to know whether or not he could trust her.

He glanced towards the bathroom door. The water was still running as he turned back towards her purse, blocking it from view should she come out. The papers weren't completely hidden, but then she hadn't expected him to already be back in the room. He pulled them from her purse—and his heart sank.

Fuck. He wanted to punch something. Wanted to put his fist through the fucking wall. Wanted to erase the evidence that was quickly mounting.

It was an offer to have her become a partner at a new sex toy company—and the amount they were giving her was beyond generous. Why? Because she was brilliant at her job? Or was it a payment of some sort for being the mole?

He heard the door open behind him. "This vibe needs a charge, so..." Her words trailed off as he turned to face her, his chest tight with hurt and anger. "What are you doing with my papers, Marshall?"

CHAPTER 20

Harper was stunned, standing there naked without even a towel to cover herself, as the man she'd fallen in love with stood there holding papers that had been in her purse. "What the hell's going on?"

"I suppose I could ask you the same thing." The papers were still fisted in Marshall's hand, his body tense and his gaze fierce. "I want a fucking explanation, Harper. Because there's a mole in my company, and my brother's trying to tell me that the evidence is all pointing in your direction."

It felt like he'd just gutted her with a jagged knife, her body shaking with the shock of his accusation. "You mean to tell me that you actually think I'm the mole?"

With his jaw clenched, he looked away from her, his eyes squeezing shut for a moment before turning his icy-cold gaze back to her, making her feel all the more naked with the sudden turn of events. "I'm trying to find evidence that would prove that you're not the mole, and instead I find this—and from a guy who works for one of the competitors that I suspect has stolen our designs."

"He wanted me to come work for him at his start-up—

and I said no. I couldn't possibly think of working for someone else when I'm in love with you—because, silly me, I'm loyal that way." When her voice cracked, it left her choking back a sob as she fled for the bathroom, locking it behind her as the tears streamed down her face. She sat there, on the cold tile floor, with her back against the door, trying to stifle her cries as her heart shattered.

"Harper..." Marshall knocked on the door, and she could tell he was just on the other side of it, which only made matters worse, since she wanted nothing more than to go back to the way things were when she'd woken up that morning. "We need to talk. Could you please come out here?"

"Fuck off, Marshall." How could he think her capable of such a thing? How could he say he loved her, and then suspect her of betraying him? She had opened up to him, she'd taken a risk by falling in love with him, especially after all she'd been through with Josh, and he'd made her believe they could be happy. "How could you think me capable of such a thing?"

"Do you fucking think this has been easy on me? Well, it hasn't, Harper. And if the evidence is all pointing to you, then you can't blame me for wanting to take a closer look." She could hear the pain in his voice, but there was also uncertainty there—uncertainty about her, about them, about their time together—and that was what killed her.

She choked back one last sob, doing her best to harden her heart against the pain, and then forced herself to pull it together. It wasn't as though she wasn't used to crumbling relationships and dealing with heartache. And now would be no different. She'd been a fool to think her life could change, to think that being happy would be anything but fleeting.

Wiping her tears away, she turned off the water, which was still filling the tub, and then got dressed, though she wasn't sure how she could face him, how she could look at him again and not be reminded that he didn't trust her. She just had to grab her things and get the hell out of there.

With her hand on the cold brass knob, she squeezed her eyes shut against the burning tears and took a deep breath to steady herself, before pulling the door open.

"Harper..." Marshall grabbed her wrist as she tried to slip past him.

"Don't touch me, Marshall." She tried to pull free of his grasp but he wasn't letting her go.

"Can we please talk about this?" He turned her towards him so she was forced to face him, though looking him in the eyes only sent her tears streaming down her face. With a sigh, his hold on her softened and then, when she didn't bolt, he reached up and cupped her face, drying her tears, his touch only fueling her emotions.

"What the hell is there to talk about if you could not only think me capable of that sort of betrayal, but actually think I'm guilty of being the mole?" Her hurt was now spiked through with anger, making her a furious mess. "I took a risk on this thing between us and opened up to you, let down the walls that were keeping me safe. And the first chance you got, at the very first opportunity to question our relationship, our love, you did just that instead of trusting what was between us—instead of trusting me."

"I was hoping to find something that proved you were innocent, Harper, so please don't go thinking the worst of me." She'd give him credit for truly looking distraught over the whole thing, but he'd broken her heart and tossed away her trust, and she didn't think she could ever look at him again and not feel crushed by the pain.

"If you wanted to prove my innocence, then maybe you should have started by speaking to me, rather than snooping through my things." She turned away from him and grabbed her things off the dresser, tossing them into her suitcase.

"Could you please stop so we can talk about this? For fuck's sake." He grasped both her hands to keep her from packing up more of her things, and sat them down on the edge of the bed so they were eye to eye, though she could only look at him through shimmering tears. "You know I didn't want to believe it was you—but when you came back from your meeting with Ben, it caught me off guard, especially when I'd just given you the passcodes to my entire life. You had access to everything, and Keane said there was evidence on your computer and your desk back at Clio. What the fuck was I supposed to do, Harper?"

"You're kidding...back in Portmore?" She felt the blood drain from her face. What the hell was going on? "I don't know what they could possibly have found, Marshall, because I have never betrayed you or Clio. I would never. And you should fucking know that."

"Well, I'm fucking sorry, Harper. I know this thing between us happened quickly, but...it's not like we really know each other all that well. You said you had problems you were dealing with. It's not exactly a stretch to think that you're desperate to get your father treatment and decided that stealing our designs would be lucrative enough to give you the cash that you need."

"And that's part of the problem—that I did fall for you

awfully fast. But I guess I was nothing but a fool to think we'd connected on a different level...one where the little things we didn't know about each other didn't matter because we were in love. That we'd still have time to discover what we didn't yet know, because we already had what was important." What a fucking idiot she'd been. "But I guess that's not going to happen, because there's nothing more to say. And just in case you're worried about firing me, don't bother. I quit."

"Harper..." He twined his fingers with hers, but even that felt halfhearted, as if he still didn't know whether she was telling him the truth. "Can we please just get back to Portmore so we can get this sorted out?"

"As far as I'm concerned, there's nothing to sort out. And I get it, Marshall. I really do. This is your company. But it doesn't make it hurt any less and it doesn't mean that things aren't over between us." She pulled free of his grasp, and with tears streaming down her face once more, she packed up the rest of her things.

Without a second glance at Marshall, she left him there and walked out the door—and he let her go.

* * *

Harper took a taxi to the airport and sat there, not quite sure what to do. She was already an emotional wreck, and the chances of her actually making it onto the plane alone and managing to control her fears were slim to none. She swiped at her tears, and with shaky hands, pulled out her cell, hating to bother anyone with her problems.

If anyone would come to her rescue, it'd be her twin cousins, Hawke and Archer. Though she was the poor relation of the family, the twins had a small fortune at their disposal, and the truth was that if she got desperate enough for her father, they were the ones she would have turned to—not stealing designs from Clio for money. As it was, they'd offered time and again, but she didn't want their money. However, right about now, she'd happily take whatever help Hawke or Archer could give her in talking her down off the ledge, her nerves about flying just too much to handle.

"Archer?" Simply hearing his voice when he answered his cell had her choking back her tears. "I need your help."

She explained that she was sort of stranded in London, attempting to get on a plane alone, and just needed him to talk to her, to distract her and tell her she could do this...just until she was calm enough to get on the plane.

"Let me come get you, Harper. I'm currently in Vienna for a gallery showing of Hawke's paintings. I could be there in just a few hours."

***

True to his word, Archer pulled Harper into his protective arms just a little while later and held her while she wept, her heart shattered and the stress of the day pushing her to her breaking point. "Come on, pumpkin. Let's get you home. You can tell me all about it during the flight."

Archer's private jet taxied the runway and then revved its engines for takeoff, sending her heart pounding inside her chest. Desperate for a distraction, she told him about Marshall and everything that happened as Archer held her in a brotherly hug, keeping her fears at bay. "I just don't understand how he could think me capable of something so awful. And if I was the mole, then why the hell would I show him my own designs?"

"Well, he's clearly an asshole and an idiot for ruining things with you. You're better off without him, as far as I'm concerned." Always protective of her, Archer was genuinely pissed off about the way Marshall had treated her. "Maybe you should come out to the island for a bit. You know Hawke would love to see you, and there's no way this prick of a boss could bother you."

Given that Archer and Hawke lived on a small private island off the coast of Maine and liked their privacy, Archer wasn't kidding about Marshall not being able to bother her—at least not without a whole lot of trouble, since the island was under the name of a dummy corporation. "I'd love to come visit—you know that. But I've got my dad to worry about, since my brother is useless. And then there's Moose, though he loves you guys."

"I know you never want any help, but I'm going to insist this time. Your dad's going to get the help he needs and you and Moose are coming for a visit." He put his hand up to stop her when she started to protest. "You no longer get a say in this, since you're too stubborn for your own good. Besides, Moose likes hanging out with Guinness, and that mutt needs a distraction."

The fact that she could so easily take off to the island only served to remind her that she no longer had a job. "How the hell did my life turn to such shit? It's even worse than it was—and that's saying something."

"We'll get you back on your feet, Harper. You have my word."

It was a sweet sentiment, but with her heart breaking as she thought of Marshall, she didn't know how she'd pull it together.

CHAPTER 21

By the time Marshall got back to Portmore, he was downright miserable. Once Harper had gone, he'd had far too much time on his hands, which meant their argument had played in an endless loop through his head. Before he even headed home, he swung by her place, though what he was hoping to accomplish he hadn't a goddamn clue.

He felt like such an ass. But what the fuck was he supposed to do? He'd only wanted to prove that she was innocent—but she'd been right. Digging through her things would have only proved her guilt or continued to feed his suspicions until he could find more evidence. Even worse, he'd let her go. He'd let her walk away, and hadn't gone after her. He'd let her find her own way back home, even if he'd held the plane as long as they'd allowed him to, with the hope she'd show up. She hadn't. And he knew how difficult flying was for her.

Marshall just needed to get to the bottom of this mess with the thefts, though first, he had to try to smooth things over with Harper. Every bone in his body told him she wasn't the mole, even if the evidence pointed to her.

With luck, Keane would have more for him to go on, because at this point, he needed some hard evidence so he'd know exactly where he stood with Harper—other than in the doghouse. And it didn't matter if things were still unresolved; he had to see her—except for the little problem of her not being home.

Panic slithered through his veins. Where the hell was she? Did she ever make it out of London, or was she still there, too panicked to get on a plane? He was such a fucking ass. How could he have abandoned her like that? Did she even have the money for a flight? Fucking hell...what had he done?

He pounded on her door again, desperately hoping she'd answer the door, that she'd been sleeping or showering. Anything other than not being home. Her cat—Moose. He'd paid for a sitter. Maybe she knew if Harper had returned.

Pulling out his phone, he tracked down the number for the sitter and dialed it, relief washing over him when she told him that she'd spoken to Harper, who was back and would no longer require her services. And no...she didn't mention that she'd be going anywhere.

Hanging up with the sitter, he dialed Harper's number. Eventually the call went to voicemail. "Harper...we need to talk. Please... Where the hell are you? Call me, okay? I'm worried about you, sunshine."

He hung up, disheartened and feeling fucking crazy.

Keane better have more answers for him, because he needed to get this mess sorted, and the longer he waited, the worse things would be with Harper. Unless, of course, Keane was right, and she was in fact the mole, even though he was having a hard time wrapping his head around it, his heart refusing to believe it.

Yet, hadn't he been mistaken about Claire? How could he trust his judgment anymore? The truth was that he couldn't. And that's why he needed hard proof that Harper was or wasn't innocent. Until then, there was little he could do.

Marshall found Keane in his office with Hadley and one of her employees, still hunting down the evidence they needed. Keane handed him a report, the mood in the room somber. "Here's the evidence we have so far. It's the dates and times she accessed the files in question."

"But how do we know it's her and not someone using her identity to log in?" He flipped through the evidence, refusing to believe it was true.

Hadley came around the desk from where she'd been working. "That is certainly a possibility, though if that is indeed what's happening here, then they'd have to have a certain amount of information, like her password, and they'd need to have easy access to her computer. I'm hoping to get access to her financial records, to see if any large deposits of money were made into any of her accounts, but...as of this moment, there's still no reason to think that it's someone other than her."

"Other than the fact that I know her and don't think she's capable of doing this. She brought me some new designs that are brilliant. Why would she do that if she was only going to turn around and sell the designs to our competitors? And someone could easily find out her password if they work in the same department as her. It wouldn't be difficult to look over her shoulder during casual conversation while she logged in." There had to be a logical explanation. "What about Claire? If there's anyone who wants to make my life miserable, it's her."

Marshall would much rather think Claire to be the guilty party than Harper. Because thinking Harper capable of such betrayal was fucking killing him.

"Dr. Foley...I know you want to believe she's innocent due to your relationship, and I promise you that we'll do all we can to make sure the proof is conclusive before giving you our final report." Hadley flipped through some more reports before continuing. "Most of the files and log-ins occurred during business hours, when she'd normally be here. So unless she called in sick but the files were still accessed, it's unlikely she'll have an alibi to prove it wasn't her, which means the evidence will still stand as her being the mole. That said, whether or not you want to press charges is up to you."

It'd be hard to get Harper to verify any of the evidence or go through the logs to help prove her innocence when he didn't know where the hell she was and she wasn't answering any of his calls. "There's one more thing I need you to do—I need you to find her. Do whatever it takes."

He turned to go when Keane put a hand on his shoulder, stopping him. "Marshall, if you need to talk... And in the meantime, we'll look to see if there's anyone else involved."

"I appreciate it." He was in no mood to stay at the office, but he needed to swing by her desk to see if there was anything she'd left behind that might tell him where she was. And he needed a copy of her personnel file. Maybe her brother or father knew where she'd gone, though he'd try her place again, on the off chance she'd shown up, though it'd likely only serve to remind him that she was long gone.

***

The department Harper had worked in really wasn't all that big, with only half a dozen employees working there, though most of them were wrapping up for the day. There was certainly a tension in the air, and he had no doubt that with Keane and Hadley investigating, rumors and speculation were likely running rampant.

"Todd, can you point me to any areas where Harper might stash away her things—and any projects or papers." Todd had been with Clio from the start and though he was the one who'd hired Harper, Marshall wasn't quite ready to tell him that Harper had quit.

"Marshall...what's going on? Keane's said very little, but they've been through all our computers and files, and I haven't heard from Harper since she left with you for the convention." Todd led the way to her desk, though he was looking rather exasperated and stressed out. "This is it for the most part, though we've also got cubbies for our jackets and things."

"I'm not sure when Harper will be back, though I'll be sure to let you know." Marshall didn't want to say too much, nor did he want to linger with Todd looking over his shoulder. "If you could get me a copy of her personnel file, I'd appreciate it."

With Todd off to get Harper's info, Marshall sat down at her desk, doing his best to ignore the tightening around his chest. Fuck...he loved her. And seeing the little personal items around her desk only reminded him of just how hard he'd fallen for her. There was a picture of her cat, Moose; a family photo of her with her dad; another of her with her friends at MIT. A few miniature metal tavern puzzles were tucked off to one side, along with a POP superhero doll of Thor, piles of sticky note pads, and various designs and schematics pinned to a corkboard.

He flipped through the calendar on her desk, though the last week or two had been left blank, no doubt due to the fact that she'd been working with him and then he'd dragged her off to London. But then he thought of something...Harper may not have been sick recently, but what if her computer had been accessed while she'd been in his office working with him on those new designs, or while he'd taken her to breakfast or to Aria's? He could check those times against that log Keane had given him, and just maybe it'd prove it couldn't have possibly been her.

It was a small ray of hope and he held onto that, ending his search of her desk, since he couldn't help but feel like he was snooping once again. Disgusted with himself and the situation in general, he got to his feet just as Todd returned with the papers he'd asked for.

"Thanks for the copy. I'll keep you updated. And in the meantime, you can start looking for a new hire." Marshall hated to have Harper's position filled, but even if she was innocent and he somehow convinced her to come back to Clio, he was still hoping she'd work with him directly, even though there was a far better chance she'd tell him to go fuck himself.

"I don't know what trouble she's gotten herself into, but...I do like her, Marshall, even if she's been a bit distant lately." It felt like Todd was trying to imply something, but he wasn't sure what, and at this point, he was in no mood to hear it.

"I'm sure we'll get to the bottom of what's going on, but she's innocent until proved otherwise." Something he, too, should have remembered.

204

Desperate to find her, he swung by her home again—only to be disappointed. Fuck. Where the hell had she gone? With his mood dark and vile, he headed home, in no state to deal with anyone else, and knowing he'd get nothing done at work if he headed back to his office.

Once at home, he poured himself a whiskey and then took a look at the papers he had in front of him, wanting to sort through the logs and other information Keane and Hadley had gathered. The log Keane had given him had a list of which files had been accessed, along with a detailed account of when and where. Yet the activity incriminating her hadn't started until just recently. He looked at the dates and information, and though everything pointed to Harper, something still felt off.

He pulled up his calendar and backtracked through the dates, from London back to the dates when Harper first started working directly with him. The files had indeed been accessed during that time period. Yet he knew Keane would point out that it'd be easy enough for her to excuse herself to use the restroom or grab a cup of coffee and then sneak back to her desk.

What Marshall needed were the dates and times he'd been with her out of the office. Using his receipts for their trips to the diner and to Aria's boutique, he matched them against the log. Yes. It was just one instance, early enough in the morning when they were at the diner, but unless she'd somehow managed to get from the diner to her desk in six minutes when it was at least a twenty-minute drive, then he had the proof he needed.

It felt so fucking good to know she hadn't betrayed him, to know that he hadn't been wrong about her. And yet it only meant that he'd truly fucked up, and she'd have every right to never forgive him.

When his phone vibrated, he made a quick grab for it, hoping it was Harper, only to have disappointment and anger flood through his veins when he realized it was Claire. He sent it to voicemail, but she called back again—and again—trying his patience. On the fifth time, he gave in and answered it. "What the hell, Claire?"

She sobbed on the other end, making him feel like a shit. "Marshall...I need you. Please...the baby..."

"What's going on? Are you okay—the baby?" He couldn't help but worry. Despite everything Claire had put him through, there was still a child involved. At least he thought there was.

"Can you come over? I don't know what to do. I think there's something wrong." The tone of her voice and her request to go over to her place had him rethinking the truth of her words.

"If there's something wrong, then you need to call your doctor, Claire." He hated to be standoffish, but the truth was that she'd never given him any documents to prove she was pregnant, even after he'd repeatedly asked for them. For all he knew, it was just another lie.

"You still don't think I'm pregnant, do you?" Nastiness laced through her words, reminding him of just how manipulative she could be.

"No—I don't. Furthermore, I think this is about the time when you'll feign losing the baby, because it doesn't actually exist." Her silence made him think he'd just hit the nail on the head. "Give up the charade, Claire, and sign the fucking divorce papers. It's not like you ever loved me anyway."

"I bet you think you're just so smart. Well, you're not. I'm going to take you down, and make sure you stay lonely and miserable, so you know that I was the best thing that ever happened to you." Stay lonely and miserable...how the fuck did she know? When he didn't say anything, she couldn't help but continue to try to bait him. "You think I don't know that the slut you've been sleeping with has left you? Took you for a ride and used you? Well, I do. Not that it's that big of a surprise."

"I'm hanging up now—and don't call me again. Don't show up. Don't fucking talk to me. If you have something to say, you do so through our lawyers. I'm filing a restraining order against you. And if you set foot on Clio property again, I'm going to have your sorry ass arrested. Are we clear? No babies, no manipulations, no tantrums. You need to stay the fuck away from me—and if you are behind the thefts at Clio, I'm going to make sure you get fitted with an orange jumpsuit—and I can fucking guarantee they don't do designer in prison."

"Marshall...please..." She sobbed out her words, but he didn't care. "I still love you. There might not be a baby, but we could try to make our marriage work again...we could try to start a family. I swear I'll be different this time. And I only did those things because I wanted to get you back. I got desperate when you kept pushing me away, so I lied...I thought we could make it work if you thought there was a baby. But then that stupid whore got in the way."

Claire was clearly delusional, though none of that mattered. The only thing he cared about was Harper—and getting her back. Claire had been manipulating him from the start, and though he might not have the evidence needed to prove Claire was behind the thefts, he knew it in his gut, now more than ever.

Not wanting to hear another word, another lie, he hung up on Claire, and then dialed Keane's number. "Look into Claire. Into her financials, into her having any sort of contact with any of the employees at Clio. She's behind this, okay? Just get the evidence we need to nail her."

"Is there any chance Claire could be working with Harper?" Keane still sounded doubtful, but Marshall knew his brother was just looking out for him.

"Not a chance in hell. Claire hates her, and I have proof it wasn't Harper. She was with me when one of the log-ins occurred on her computer. And there's more... The baby? Yeah...it never existed. Claire was lying the whole time."

"Fucking hell, Marshall...I can't believe that bitch would go to such lengths. But this is good, right? And...I'm glad it's not Harper. She seemed nice—and you seemed happy. I'm just sorry it got messed up." Marshall could hear the regret in his brother's voice, though it was a small consolation. "I'll keep you updated. We'll get to the bottom of this. You have my word."

CHAPTER 22

Harper tried to distract herself from the ache in her heart, but to no avail. It'd been over a week since she last saw Marshall, and though he continued to call and leave messages, she couldn't bring herself to listen to them. Whatever he had to say no longer mattered, since it was clear he didn't trust her or have any faith in what they'd felt for each other.

And why should he? They may have known each other for close to a year, but they'd only been dating a short while—if you could even call it dating. More like falling in love while fucking. Because there was no denying that she had indeed fallen in love with him, even if it proved to be a huge mistake.

Harper glanced over at Hawke as he walked into the room with Guinness, who raced past him to sit at her side, his tail wagging furiously as if he was seeing her for the first time in days. She gave the big black dog a scratch on the head, appreciating how the simple act of petting him always seemed to calm her. "Are you two heading out?"

"I am—and you're coming with us. Guinness wants to run on the shore and it'll do you some good to get out of the house. You're starting to look like a sea captain's wife, constantly sitting by the window, looking forlorn as you wait for your love to return to you on the tide." As an artist—and a well accomplished one at that—Hawke always had a way of painting a picture, even if it was with his words. It was as if he could somehow see the story in every scene, and it was just waiting for him to bring it to life with a stroke of his brush.

The depression that kept threatening to take her since London loomed around her like a poisonous fog, clinging to her very soul, and she knew firsthand how easy it'd be to let it take hold of her, just like it had after her breakup with Josh. So when her cousin took her hand in his and pulled her to her feet, she let him.

Though it was a bright and sunny day in early May, they were in Maine, and with the wind blowing in off the ocean, it was still blustery and cold. She snuggled deeper into her jacket as she walked the beach with Hawke, who was certainly the quieter of the twins, though they never really discussed his past. They may have grown up in a wealthy family, but it hadn't spared them a decade of heartache and abuse.

She couldn't even fathom what the twins had been through, and was well aware that she didn't know the whole story. But what she did know was that Hawke...he'd taken the brunt of the abuse to spare his brother, and it had changed him forever.

"What will you do, pumpkin?" She loved that they still used their nickname for her from when they were kids. "Although you know you're welcome to stay here as long as you'd like. I'm sure we could even put you on the payroll if you'd like, since Archer has more than he can handle on his plate trying to handle the media, sales, and gallery showings."

"I appreciate it, Hawke." She didn't know what she'd have done if she'd been left to deal with her nightmare of a life in Portmore. "You and Archer mean the world to me, though my dad will eventually be getting out of rehab and I want to be there for him when he gets back. That won't be for some time, though, so I can stay a bit longer."

"What about this guy—Marshall? I'd like to say he doesn't deserve you, but...you've been downright miserable." Hawke picked up the stick that Guinness dropped at his feet and tossed it as far as he could, so the big black mutt went tearing across the beach. "Will you give him another chance?"

"I just don't know, Hawke."

"Well, I hate to say it, but you might need to make a decision sooner rather than later, though I'm not sure Archer will put the bridge down to let him pass. And then there's the little matter of him getting past the shotgun." He tilted his head towards the bridge that linked the island with the mainland and the car driving over it.

Clearly, the sign stating that the bridge and island were private property hadn't been much of a deterrent to Marshall. Not that he'd be getting far with part of the bridge up.

"I don't think I can bear to see him, Hawke." She already sounded panicky.

"You don't have to do anything you don't want to, Harper. You know that." He shifted towards her, his hands stuffed in his pockets as he gave her a shrug, his broad shoulders sheltering her from the wind. "But...miserable as you've been, I think you should at least hear him out. If for no other reason than to get some closure so you can move past this."

"I know you're right...I just don't know if I can bear to see him again." Her gut was already in knots. Yet, despite the heartache, despite the hurt he'd caused, she found herself drawn to Marshall, her pulse skittering away at the mere thought of him.

"Did you truly love him, Harper?" Hawke tilted his head as if catching every nuance of light and color in her face.

"Yeah...I did. Still do, I'm afraid." It'd be a hell of a lot easier if she didn't. "But that doesn't excuse what he did."

"No, pumpkin. It doesn't. But you never know what he might have to say for himself. And this way it'll keep you from questioning whether or not you made the right decision." He whistled to the dog, and started heading back to the house, slowing his long stride so she could easily keep up with him. "Just remember...you're welcome to stay here as long as you'd like. It's been great having you around, since it's just Archer and me most days."

She knew that was an understatement. Hawke's abuse had left him withdrawn from the world, putting Archer in charge of selling Hawke's art and going to gallery showings, although they certainly didn't need the money. She supposed that as an artist, there was an element of wanting to share the beauty he'd created, even if Hawke never got to see the reactions to his work firsthand.

Given that they were identical, she knew that the outside world didn't realize that Hawke was a twin, especially since he was so reclusive. As an added measure of privacy, he also sold his paintings under a different name entirely, one

Archer also adopted when dealing with the outside world. The twins were essentially one person, as far as the outside world was concerned.

Slipping her hand around Hawke's arm, she looked up at her cousin, thinking he was so handsome, talented, and kind—and thinking it such a waste that so much of his childhood and innocence had been stolen from him. "I wish you'd get out more, Hawke. There's so much to see and do."

"Maybe someday."

CHAPTER 23

Marshall had to give Harper credit. If her plan had been to get away from him and make it nearly impossible for him to find her, then she'd certainly done one hell of a job. Not only were her cousins and everything they owned well off the radar, they also lived nearly four hours from Portmore on a private island off the coast of Maine. He was just lucky that Hadley was damn good at her job, and somehow managed to find them.

He didn't know what Harper's cousins did for a living, but if the old Victorian mansion and private island were anything to go by, money wasn't an issue. No wonder she said she had other options than stealing Clio's designs for money if she got desperate. The fact that he'd thought her capable of such things...he was such a fucking ass.

Halfway across the bridge, he came to a section of it that was raised like a drawbridge, preventing him going any farther. He threw his car in park, but before he could get out to deal with the intercom that would have him pleading his case to a metal box, the bridge started to lower.

His hands tightened on the steering wheel as he tried to wrangle his thoughts. There was so much to tell Harper—

and he'd do everything he could to get her back. He'd been a miserable wreck since she left, and not having her in his life just wasn't an option.

By the time he pulled up in front of the massive home, which was reminiscent of the Newport mansions both in style and age, there was a man already standing at the front door, a shotgun at his side. And though he didn't feel like getting shot, there was no fucking way he was leaving without Harper.

"You have some balls showing up here after what you put Harper through." The man was tall with a muscular build, in his late twenties, with dark hair and fiercely blue eyes, though whether this was Archer or Hawke, Marshall hadn't a clue. Nor did he know how to get past the shotgun if Harper didn't want to come out to speak to him.

"I'm just asking her to hear me out—and I'm not leaving until she's done just that." Fuck...they were multiplying. The other twin came out and stood by his brother's side so Marshall now had two of them to deal with. "I don't care how many of you there are—I'm not going."

"Are you sure about that?" The shotgun got cocked, but Marshall held his ground.

"Harper!" He called out as loud as he could, hoping she could hear him through the massive oak doors. "For fuck's sake—just talk to me. Please."

The second twin stepped forward, tension in his every move as if he was ready to pounce—not that Marshall cared. He could take care of himself, and he wasn't going anywhere without Harper. "What exactly are your intentions? Because you've put her through more than enough already, and if you're here just to stir up trouble, you can take your sorry ass and your accusations the fuck out of here."

"It was never my intention to hurt her, but this discussion is between me and her—not the two of you." He didn't care if he pissed them off. But before things could escalate and get ugly, the door opened and Harper stepped out, the wind catching her dark hair and streaking it across her pale skin.

His heart pounded inside his chest at the mere sight of her, his body moving towards her as if drawn by an invisible force—and fuck...she wouldn't even look at him, as if it was too much to bear. "There's nothing to say, Marshall."

He took several more steps towards her, doing his best to shrug past the twins, needing to be with her, needing to hold her in his arms again. "That's where you're wrong. Just hear me out, sunshine...please. And then if you still want me to go, I will."

"Fine...I'll hear you out since you came all this way, but then you're leaving." Harper reassured her cousins and though they stepped aside, neither of them was looking all that happy about it.

When she started walking towards one of the gardens, he stepped to her side and followed her, forcing him to fight the urge to pull her into his arms and kiss her until all their problems dissipated in the heat between them. Once they rounded the house and had a bit of privacy, she slowed to a stop and turned to face him.

Tears shimmered in her eyes—but only for a moment, as if the wind were at fault rather than the small fact that he'd been a complete jerk to her. Or maybe it was because she was done with him and she wouldn't be wasting any more tears on what they once had together. "Why did you come here, Marshall? Because if you think there's anything left between us, let me just stop you right there."

"You know that's a lie, Harper. We might be the two most miserable people on the planet right about now, but the reason we're miserable is because we're apart when we should be together." She could deny it all she wanted but they both knew it was nothing but the truth.

She scoffed at him with a shake of her head. "If that was the case, then you'd think you might actually trust me—which you don't. And don't get me wrong—I get it. There's a mole at Clio and you've been desperately trying to get to the bottom of it."

"There was a mole, or rather, moles, Harper. We caught them. That's the other reason I'm here. I wanted you to know that Claire was behind it all. She had several of my employees on her payroll—Todd included." Yet again, Claire had somehow managed to get people he worked with to betray him, for money this time instead of sex, though whether they were also sleeping together, he didn't know—nor did he care.

"Todd? No...I can't believe it." Any walls she'd put up came crashing down, her emotions written all of her face.

"I'm sorry, Harper, I really am. But he confessed to all of it. It was how Claire was able to plant the evidence that would make us suspect you. It was also why the evidence only recently started pointing in your direction, though Todd may have been planning to use you as a scapegoat all along, since he knew Ben worked for Titan and you were friends. And then once Claire realized we were together, she knew she could come between us and hurt me further by making me think it was you." Marshall felt horrible that he'd put Harper through this—and he felt like an ass for letting Claire manipulate him yet again and allowing her to come between them.

"I guess she did a damn good job of it." This time, her tears spilled over, as if it was finally all too much to hold together.

Hating to see her upset, he pulled her into his arms as she wept, ignoring her struggles to get free. She finally gave up and settled in his arms as he held her tight, doing his best to soothe her until her tears finally slowed. "Harper...I was a fucking idiot, and I swear I'll do everything I can to make this up to you, to fix what I screwed up. And I know I screwed up. I know I should have never doubted you...never doubted what was between us."

She pounded his chest in frustration. "How could you, Marshall? Do you know how hard it was for me to open up to you, to let you into my heart? I trusted you not to hurt me, and you betrayed that trust in practically the same breath as the one you used to tell me you loved me."

"I didn't want to believe it, Harper—and I wasn't looking for evidence to incriminate you, but to prove to Keane that you were innocent. But...I had been so incredibly wrong about Claire, and I didn't trust my judgment anymore." He let out a deep sigh, still hating himself that he'd let Claire manipulate him all this time. "My issues got in the way of what I knew to be the truth. And I never should have let you go. But Harper...being apart just isn't an option. I love you more than anything—and I want you to come home with me."

"I don't know that I can, Marshall." She shrugged out of his embrace and took a step back, distancing herself from him.

He snagged her hand, refusing to let her go. He couldn't. Not when she was the only thing that mattered. "Did you mean it when you said you loved me?"

She glared at him, her blue eyes fierce. "Damn it, Marshall. You know I did."

"Then I'm asking for one more chance. Come back to Portmore. Because what we have hasn't been given a fair chance, and there's no fucking way I'm giving up on us. I fucking love you, Harper." And then he was closing the distance between them, cupping her face in his hands and catching her mouth in a kiss as he hauled her body to his.

Her struggles ceased as she softened in his arms, their kiss deepening until she planted her hands on his chest and pushed him away, though he managed to keep his hold on her. "Kissing me doesn't change the fact that you thought I'd betrayed you—and you let me walk away. You knew how upset I was, knew how difficult it was for me to get on that plane, and you still let me go. You continued to think that I was behind the thefts."

"I fucked up, Harper—I know I did. And maybe I don't deserve another chance. But you know what? I'm going to ask for it anyway because I'm fucking miserable without you. I can't think straight, and I can't get you out of my head...out of my heart." Now wasn't the time to hold anything back. Not if he had any hope of her giving him another chance. "I swear, I've never felt this way about anyone—not even close. I love you, Harper—just like you love me—and I'll spend the rest of my days making it up to you, making you happy. You're my everything, and leaving here without you isn't an option—even if your cousins will likely blow a hole through me for attempting to take you home."

"They are just a little protective of me." The slightest smile slipped onto her lips, and he swore he could feel her resolve softening just a little. "I suppose I'd rather not get my cousins tossed in jail for murder, though I suspect they could do a pretty good job of burying your body or feeding it to the fishes."

"I know I fucked up, Harper. That's not even a question. But I need you to give me—give us—another chance. Because if you truly love me, then you know that being apart will do nothing but destroy us both." He cupped her cheek, and bent his head to hers, breathing in deep so her familiar scent filled his head. "I love you, Harper...more than anything, I love you."

"You know I love you, Marshall—but you questioned it, questioned me and my integrity—and that fucking hurt." The pain in her voice killed him...yet, when he nuzzled her, she didn't pull away but rather leaned into him, as if she too couldn't resist the pull between them.

"Come on, Harper...you have to head home sometime. And I swear I'll do everything I can to make things right between us." It might be a reach, but they'd been flirting over coffee and donuts since he first met her, and it just might be enough of a sentimental excuse to get her to agree to come with him. "And just in case you're on the fence, I know of this amazing donut shop on the way home."

Her eyes narrowed as if mulling things over—or just to ensure he suffered just a little while longer. "Do they have Boston Cream?"

"You bet, sunshine."

"Not that this means you're forgiven."

CHAPTER 24

Harper still couldn't believe she was letting Marshall take her home. Things were still tense between them, though that was probably her fault, since she'd clammed up during the car ride, not really trusting that her emotions wouldn't get the better of her. She needed to keep a clear head if she had any hope of thinking about the situation logically. Because one thing was sure— it'd be far too easy to give in to what was between them and get her heart broken again.

Marshall pulled off the highway and, after a short drive down some back roads, pulled into a parking lot and shifted in his seat to face her, twining his fingers with hers. "Donuts—just as promised. Will Moose be okay if we leave him for a few minutes to grab a bite?"

It was sweet of him to think of her cat. "Yeah...he doesn't mind the carrier as long as he has his blanket to sleep on, and the temperature is fine so that's not an issue either."

"Harper...I truly am sorry for hurting you." He cupped her cheek, his eyes pleading with her as his touch made it impossible to pull away from him, her pulse racing as she fought the urge to lean in and kiss him.

As if they'd shared the same thought, he bent his head to hers and caught her mouth in a kiss, slow and sweet at first, but with a building intensity as she gave in to what was between them. Things might be far from perfect, but she'd been a wretched mess without him, and after what felt like a lifetime of misery, she couldn't deal with any more of it. She wanted to be happy, damn it. And she had been happy with Marshall, even if it had been short-lived.

By the time she managed to pull away from him, her body was aching to have back what was once between them, and her head was spinning as tears stung her eyes. "Why does everything always have to be so difficult? Why couldn't we just be happy? Between the thefts at Clio and your pregnant ex plotting against you every step of the way, I don't know why I'm surprised that it all went to hell."

"I can't believe I forgot to tell you. Claire...she's not pregnant. It was all just another lie to manipulate me." Upon hearing his words, Harper let out a breath she didn't even realize she'd been holding. "Keane and the security firm we hired are still gathering evidence for the thefts, but we'll be able to press charges if we want to pursue it legally."

"I can't believe she'd go to such lengths." No wonder Marshall had become so paranoid, especially when he'd trusted Claire enough to actually marry her—only to have her cheat on him, manipulate and lie to him, steal from him. After all Claire put him through, could Harper really blame Marshall for wanting proof that she hadn't been involved, especially when there was evidence pointing in her direction?

"I should have known it was her all along, Harper." With his brow furrowed, he shook his head, clearly angry with himself. "I should never have let anything come between us, let alone Claire—and I swear, I'll do whatever it takes to make things right between us."

She could see the pain and regret in his eyes, the worry in his face, and it killed her. They had been so happy—and they'd let outside forces tear them apart. They'd let Claire, of all people, manipulate them and come between them, and it suddenly felt like they were letting her win.

Harper couldn't let that happen—not when she and Marshall had been so happy. And just like that, she felt all her hurt and anger melt away, replaced by the possibility of being happy once again.

With her pulse racing, she took a deep breath to try to steady her nerves. "Well, if you want to make things right between us, then I suppose you can start with that donut you promised me."

"You drive a hard bargain, sweet girl, but I think I can manage it."

***

When Marshall kissed her again, he tasted like chocolate and vanilla cream, and she swore he seemed determined to keep kissing her until there was nothing else between them but the love they had for each other. He'd gotten her home—with a few extra donuts for the road—and with Moose fed and on the loose, there was nothing else to focus on but each other.

"Tell me you forgive me, Harper." His words danced over her skin as his hot mouth trailed down her neck, sending a shiver of need through her and straight to her core. And when he raked his teeth over her pulse, she couldn't help but lean into him, his body hard against hers, as if reminding her of all he was capable of.

"I do...I forgive you. But don't you ever do that to me again." She'd never survive another heartbreak.

"Never. You have my word." Hauling her off her feet, he kissed her as she wrapped her legs around his waist, his stiff cock pressing against her heat and making her clit throb in time to her heartbeat.

She knotted her fingers in his thick, dark hair, her tongue dancing over his, deepening their kiss as he carried her down the hall and to her room. Lowering her to the bed, he tore her top up over her head and then yanked off his own t-shirt, exposing ripped abs, a broad chest, and strong, muscular arms. Sitting up, she ran her hands over his sides to his back, pressing kisses along his stomach so his muscles tensed under her lips.

Clearly impatient, he flicked open the clasp on her bra and she tossed it aside, before making quick work of the button and zipper on his jeans, desperate to free his hard cock. Wrapping her hands around his girth, she stroked him and then ran her tongue along his length and flicked the head of his cock, licking at the salty gem of pre-cum that glistened there.

He let out a groan as she wrapped her lips around his cock and sucked him, slipping her lips up and down his shaft as she stroked him. But then he was pulling away, leaving her to protest, as he pushed her onto her back, and yanked her jeans and panties off in one go before ridding himself of what was left of his own clothing. "After a week without you, I'm not going to last if you keep that up. And right about now I need to bury myself deep inside you, need to feel your body wrapped around me—and I need to take you hard enough to erase our week apart."

Already shifting between her legs, he thrust into her, skin to skin, burying himself fully inside her with a single thrust as he covered her body with his and plundered her mouth in a greedy kiss. His thrusts were slow but purposeful, so she felt each one down to the marrow of her bones, and into the depths of her soul, the intensity between them all-consuming, like flying too close to the sun.

She could think of nothing but him, his cock filling her, stretching her tight as he rocked his hips into her and then rolled them to catch her clit, each stroke pushing her closer to the edge. Continuing to take her, to claim her as his, he raked his teeth down her neck, each nip and bite lighting up in a flicker of pain that quickly turned to pleasure, heightening everything she was feeling and spurring her on. And when he teased her nipple and nipped at it, sucking it into his mouth, she bucked into him, trying to quicken their pace, the energy inside her building.

It was all too much: their time apart, the love she felt for him, the happiness he was offering her…and then she was coming, crying out his name, as he covered her face in kisses. "I love you, Harper…with everything that I am."

Her body quivered below his weight as he slowed his thrusts, milking the last of her orgasm from her body, her breathing still heavy even as she found the words and emotions she'd tried so hard to ignore. "I love you, too."

He pulled out of her, biting back a needy moan as he grabbed her hips and flipped her onto her hands and knees, burying himself deep inside her once more with a hard thrust that had her crying out, her body already so sensitive from just having come. With his back pressed to hers, he propped himself up with one arm as his other wrapped across her chest and his fingers gently slipped around her neck, pulling her head back to him as he drove into her, her body pinned in place by his muscular form.

His name was like a mantra on her lips as he claimed her body, heart, and soul as his, pushing her towards that delicious edge once more. She could think of nothing but him and the love that was between them, as he drove into her, his mouth at her ear so his warm breath tickled her skin and sent a shiver shimmying down her spine. "Mine. You're mine and no one else's. And you...you've had my heart from the very start, Harper. Now come for me. One more time."

And so she did just that, her orgasm torn from her body as he joined her, each thrust like a punctuation as his cock pulsed deep inside her, filling her with hot cum, their hearts and souls now one. "I love you, Marshall. With all my heart, I truly do."

"And you, sweet girl, are my everything."

CHAPTER 25

I t'd been two months since Marshall went to Maine and convinced Harper to give him another chance, and he couldn't possibly be happier, especially since she and Moose had moved in with him. He'd even convinced her to come back to Clio so they could continue working on their projects together and kick the competition's ass, since their designs were now safe, having managed to eliminate every person Claire had bribed.

With enough evidence to go after Claire for corporate espionage—something the authorities were taking very seriously—the courts not only granted him a divorce, they had also thrown out her appeal, putting an end to any claim she'd made for Clio. He could now leave Claire and their miserable history behind him, and get a fresh start on a new life with Harper.

He'd give Harper a little more time, not wanting to rush her and scare her off, but he'd already bought her the most exquisite engagement ring, and when the time was right, he'd propose and do everything in his power to make sure she said yes.

Harper settled into his arms in the back of the limo as

they drove through Boston, and he undid the bowtie on his tux, before pressing a kiss to her forehead. "You looked gorgeous tonight, sunshine."

She'd worn a beautiful gown of shimmering silver that hugged every curve, making it nearly impossible for him to keep his hands off her. Shifting in his arms, she looked up at him, a content smile on her lips. "And you were easily the most handsome guy there."

"Where the hell was Keane though? He was supposed to be there tonight." It'd been another charity event, co-hosted with the Rykers, and though he knew Keane didn't love going to anything too formal, he wasn't one not to show up when he said he would. Marshall had tried calling him, but all his calls had gone straight to voicemail.

"You know what he's like...he's always busy with one thing or another. But if you're worried, we should swing by his place and check in on him." Harper pressed a kiss to his throat, her lips soft and warm, making it so he could think of nothing but getting her home and naked.

"It's nearly one in the morning. I'll swing by there first thing tomorrow if he hasn't called or shown up."

He didn't get the chance. The call came at nearly four in the morning. Marshall shook the sleep off as his heart hammered in his head, the unexpected call sending a jolt of adrenaline through his system though his thoughts were still thick with sleep. "I'm sorry...can you repeat that? I don't understand...Keane's been arrested?"

What the hell had his brother gone and done?

THE END

*** I hope you enjoyed Passion. Keane's story, Obsession, the next book in The Billionaire's Seduction Series, is now. Also available is Hawke and Archer's story, Forbidden. For updates, please sign up for my newsletter via my website, and as always, reviews are greatly appreciated, if you're so inclined. — Best, Cali ***

HAVE YOU READ THEM ALL?

Book Series by Cali MacKay

The Billionaire's Seduction Series

Passion

Obsession

Scandal

Temptation

The Billionaire's Temptation Series

Seduction and Surrender

Submission and Surrender

Love and Surrender

Deception and Surrender

Ravage and Surrender

Forbidden – The Townsend Twins Series

Parts 1 - 4

The Silver Moon Pack Series
Greyson

Part 1 - 4

A Maine Island Romance Series

One Sweet Summer

For Love or Treasure

Sweet Danger

The Highland Heart Series

The Highlander's Hope

A Highland Home

A Highland Heist

Also available as The Highland Heart Collection

The Pirate and the Feisty Maid Series

Part One, Two and Three only available as a boxset

Jack—A Grim Reaper Romance

Made in the USA
Middletown, DE
03 March 2016